SFGRA

# Beware a Wronged Avenger

An army patrol led by Lieutenant Shadrak Pickett is making its way through the Pioneer Mountains in south-west Montana. Its purpose is to deliver the monthly payroll to Fort Wisdom. But everything changes when a solitary traveller is encountered who claims his horse has died from a snake bite. The man asks for a ride to the next settlement. Being an old colleague of officer Pickett, the request is granted.

But Jake Rankin's plan is to steal the payroll in such a way that Pickett takes the blame. A cunning means of deception by the brigand ruins Pickett's career by having him drummed out of the army for cowardice. Can the wronged man avenge his disgrace and bring Rankin back to face justice? A quirk of fate in which innocence and guilt become entangled must be overcome for him to succeed.

# Beware a Wronged Avenger

Ethan Flagg

**A Black Horse Western**

ROBERT HALE

© Ethan Flagg 2020
First published in Great Britain in 2020

ISBN 978-0-7198-3143-0

The Crowood Press
The Stable Block
Crowood Lane
Ramsbury
Marlborough
Wiltshire SN8 2HR

www.bhwesterns.com

Robert Hale is an imprint
of The Crowood Press

The right of Ethan Flagg to be identified as
author of this work has been asserted by him
in accordance with the Copyright, Designs
and Patents Act 1988

Typeset by
Simon and Sons ITES Services Pvt Ltd
Printed and bound in Great Britain by
4Bind Ltd, Stevenage, SG1 2XT

# ONE

## ENCOUNTER FROM THE PAST

Two days out from the town of Dillon, Montana, the four-man army detail had left behind the valley of the Beaverhead flatlands. Ahead of them lay the ominous climb up through densely packed slopes of pine and fir cloaking the arduous trek through the Pioneer Mountains. Their next camp would be at Badger Pass. Beyond this gap in the mountains, it was a straight run down along the Big Hole Valley following the left bank of Grasshopper Creek to their destination at Fort Wisdom.

This was a regular run for Lieutenant Shadrak Pickett. His mission was to collect the fort's monthly payroll. It was his third such trip. All the others had gone smoothly with no hitches, and there was no reason to suppose this one would be any different. No ominous signs of trouble had come from the Sioux Indian tribes due to the firm grip enforced by the occupying military forces. Since the signing of the treaty with Red Cloud in 1868, an uneasy peace had settled over the territory.

The tribes, however, were again becoming restive. More and more gold prospectors were drifting into the territory. But so far no serious incident had caused the Indians to rise up and attack the white invaders of their tribal lands. However, this peace was illusory, merely a chimera, one that would lead to violent change over the coming years, abruptly culminating in 1876. That was the year when the infamous defeat of General Custer at the Battle of the Little Big Horn unleashed a national outcry to bring the Indians to heel.

But that was four years in the future. On this June day of 1872 Shad Pickett was riding at the head of his small detachment. He tugged his hat down to shade out the harsh sun, constantly alert for any perceived threat. For this was no ordinary trip. Apart from a military presence to guard the regular payroll, an extra passenger had been permitted to accompany the detail. Millie Jefferson was going to join her husband, Colonel George Jefferson, the commanding officer of Fort Wisdom.

The lieutenant was more than a little aware of this added responsibility resting on his broad shoulders. 'Keep your eyes open, men,' he rasped, not for the first time since they had entered the confines of the foothills. 'I heard in Dillon that some young buck called Crazy Horse is living up to his name by inciting

the Sioux to rebel. We can't be too blasted careful.'
He immediately realized his error in using strong
language, and apologized to the lady riding up front
alongside Private Starkey. The driver was struggling
to hide a smirk while he deftly handled the reins.
'Pardon my language, ma'am,' said Pickett, touching
his hat. 'It just slipped out.'

'That's all right, lieutenant,' Millie replied with
a broad smile. Her blue eyes flashed, causing the
stalwart officer to blush. 'Being a soldier's wife, I've
heard plenty worse.' Although old enough to be the
officer's mother, Millie Jefferson was still an attractive
woman. The officer couldn't help but notice the sly
glances passing between the men.

Accordingly he was relieved to notice the sun glint-
ing on something that had fallen into the bed of the
wagon. He was glad of the distraction. Peering closer
he saw that it was a gold-leafed brooch. He leaned
down and picked it up. 'Reckon this must be your'n,
ma'am,' he observed in his distinctive Texan brogue
while admiring the valuable ornament with an appre-
ciative gaze. 'You sure don't want to lose such a fine
piece of jewellery out here.'

Millie gasped, her large eyes wide with surprise.
'My, my! What a careless girl I am! George would
be mighty peeved if'n I lost this,' she was babbling
in embarrassment, and quickly fastened the brooch
back in place. 'It was a present from his mother on
our wedding day. A family heirloom handed down
through generations. I am in your debt, sir.'

The incident was unexpectedly cut short by the startled intervention of Private Starkey. 'Looks like we've gotten us a visitor, sir.' Pickett's eye followed the direction of the trouper's pointing arm. And there, perched on a saddle at the side of the trail some fifty yards up ahead, sat a single figure. The officer held up a hand, bringing the detail to a halt. His probing gaze searched the dense stand of trees to see if there were any other potentially unwelcome travellers in the vicinity, but nothing of a human variety met his scrutiny. Only a couple of deer, alerted to this alien presence, were spotted disappearing into the forest.

For a long minute Pickett studied the man, who had now risen to his feet. The jasper did not appear to harbour any threat. And the saddle seemed to indicate that his horse had suffered some form of accident, casting him afoot. Nevertheless, Pickett's hand rested on the gun butt of his army-issue .44 Remington revolver as he nudged his horse up the trail to confront the individual.

It was the other man who spoke first. 'I sure am glad to see you fellas,' he said, heaving a sigh of relief. 'I been stuck here since yesterday. A rattler did for my horse. I'd sure appreciate a lift back to civilization…' He paused in mid flow, a startled expression coming over his stubble-coated features. 'Well, ain't this my lucky day?' he declared, an oily smile spreading over his craggy face. 'Never figured to meet up with you again. Not after our last… erm… should we say, thorny encounter.' Then his eyes rested pointedly on the two pips gracing the officer's shoulders. 'I see our past disagreement hasn't done you any harm. Promoted to full lieutenant, eh? Life appears to have been much kinder to you than it has to me.'

The man's peevish tone made Pickett stiffen in the saddle. Now it was his turn to display puzzlement as he carefully inspected this perplexing character. How did the guy know him? 'Surely you haven't forgotten your old sergeant?' the man queried. 'After all, it was only six months ago that you ruined my career.'

A humourless smirk left it for Pickett to work out the unsettling details. '*Sergeant Rankin!*' Recognition of his old second-in-command struck Pickett like the kick from a loco mule. Shock registered on his ashen face, much to Rankin's delight. But the footloose traveller's amusement instantly faded as he gave a timely reminder of the true situation. '*Ex*-sergeant Rankin, as I'm sure you well recall... sir,' the man reminded his listener.

An instant flashback brought the disquieting facts of their clash to mind. On the poignant night in question, Second Lieutenant Shad Pickett had been on guard duty. In the middle watch while rounding a corner in a remote part of Fort Wisdom, he had accidently chanced upon his trusted sergeant pilfering the quartermaster's store.

The officer's unscheduled visit to the store block had been to place an order for the latest Springfield rifles. The important job had been unfortunately forgotten during the day, and at that late hour the building was locked up. But he knew that a wagon was leaving at first light for the local armoury based at Dillon. An official docket signed by the adjutant and left on the quartermaster sergeant's desk would be sufficient.

Rankin was spotted surreptitiously leaving the store toting a bulging sack. Just in time, Pickett pulled back out of sight. The sergeant's shifty manner instantly raised his suspicions that something illicit was afoot. As such he cautiously followed the non-com into the town of Wisdom to determine what the sly jasper was up to. The puzzled officer dogged his quarry, making sure to keep a safe distance without losing sight of the dishonest rogue.

The pursuit led him into a part of the town not frequented by the more affluent citizens of Wisdom. Mean shacks abounded, and the odious smell from a pig holding stung the back of his throat.

Pickett was shocked and tormented in equal measure. He had never for one minute considered that the stalwart trouper was nought but a common thief. Rankin had not only been regarded as a trusted back-up soldier, but also a friend. Such a liaison was rare in the western army, one that was not encouraged by the senior authorities. Discovery of the truth shook Pickett's faith in human nature to the core.

As a consequence the steadfast officer was dumbfounded, and left in a quandary as to what he should do. If he were to arrest the man and have him brought before a tribunal, the latter would likely have him flogged, then sent to a punishment unit.

The alternative was to have him quietly transferred to another company. The one thing he could not do was ignore this dereliction of duty. And he sadly concluded that this was likely not the first time it had occurred.

Rankin met up with three sour-faced brigands, and then proceeded to sell the stolen goods, much to his friend's dismay. A brief conversation took place, after which the dishonest transaction was completed. Money and goods changed hands, after which the conniving participants disappeared into the night. Only Rankin stayed where he was, counting the green-backs with a lascivious grin pasted on to his face.

The stunned watcher had been placed in an awkward position. What should he do? Consideration of the matter was taken out of his hands by a drunk staggering into him from behind. 'What in thunder-ation...!' The drink-induced exclamation immediately exposed the officer's position of concealment as Pickett found himself pushed out into the open, while the soused drunk staggered off, totally unheeding of his unpropitious action.

Rankin was instantly alerted and turned to face this potential threat. 'Who's there?' he hissed, stiffening his posture. A gun suddenly appeared in his hand. 'Show yourself, or eat lead!' At that precise moment the moon chose to emerge from where it had been hiding behind a bank of fluffy cumulus clouds. An ethereal glow swept away the shadows to reveal Rankin's commanding officer, and the sergeant relaxed on recognizing his superior.

'Oh, it's you, Shad,' he said, relief easing out the tight lines etched across his leathery features. 'You gave me a shock there. I thought some night owl was trying to hustle me.' He slipped the revolver back into its holster. 'What are you doing in this part of town, buddy? I didn't figure it to be the kind of stamping ground officers generally frequent.'

Pickett remained tight-lipped. Rankin was a cool customer all right. He clearly figured that his so-called pal was tarred with the same brush, and would want a cut of the proceeds. But Lieutenant Shad Pickett was not to be bought off, as Rankin soon learned. The hard-eyed expression told the thief that his close association with this go-by-the-book officer was now dead in the water: his underhanded thieving had effectively seen to that. Both men faced each other, the sergeant becoming aware that this was no chance encounter.

'So why are you down here...lieutenant?' The question was punched out, biting and accusatory.

'Don't "buddy" me, Rankin,' Pickett rasped, breathing deep to control his growing anger. 'I saw what you did back there.' The curt rejoinder was flat, devoid of feeling. 'Stealing from the company store, then selling the loot to a bunch of conniving lowlifes. How shameful can you get?'

Rankin hawked out a nervous laugh, but no hint of humour was visible on the ashen face. 'You got this all wrong, lieutenant,' he blustered, raising his hands. 'It was just a little bit of personal business I was conducting. Nothing illegal in it.'

Now it was Pickett's turn to toss out a brittle snort of disdain. 'Don't try and deny it. I watched you sneaking out of the store toting a full sack. My problem now is what to do about it.' His own gun was now drawn and aimed at the culprit's stomach. Time hung heavy in the cool night air as both men held each other's gaze.

'You could accept a half share of what I got for those goods.' Rankin was a guy who figured that every man had his price – but he soon realized that Shad Pickett was no such weakling. The sardonic expression on the lieutenant's face was enough to inform the thief that his proposal had fallen on deaf ears. Shad Pickett was a company man through and through, and Rankin should have known it. Tough and dependable in battle, impartial when dealing with insubordination, and most definitely no walk-over when it came to bending the rules. 'But I guess that ain't your way, is it lieutenant?'

No answer was required, nor was one given – except for an ultimatum. Shad Picket had made his decision. 'You've betrayed my trust, Jake,' Pickett observed with some regret. 'And for that I should toss you to the wolves. But because of our previous association, I'm prepared to give you the chance to go quietly. You saved my life on Lodge Tail Ridge when Little Wolf attacked us back in sixty-seven, and I don't forget that sort of bravery in a hurry.' He paused to draw breath. 'So I won't report you.'

The thief's attempted thanks were shrugged off. 'But tomorrow first thing, I expect you to request

13

a transfer. A notice went up in the company office today for troopers to garrison a new fort that's just been completed at Willow Creek over in the Madison Valley.'

Another pause followed to allow the accused time to consider his options. Pickett helped him to decide with a virulent threat. 'Refuse my offer and I'll throw the book at you. And I can assure you that a punishment unit is no Sunday school picnic.'

'So what reason am I to give for requesting a transfer?' Rankin snapped back. 'I've been with this outfit from the beginning.'

Pickett responded with a scoff laced with acid mockery: 'I'm sure a smart guy like you will figure out some appropriate excuse. I'll look in after morning parade to check you've kept your part of the deal. Don't disappoint me.' And with that he backed off down the side alley. No way was he going to turn his back on this back-stabbing turncoat. A solid friendship had been well and truly buried.

Next morning Sergeant Rankin was absent from parade. An enquiry from Corporal Livesey revealed that the absentee had reported sick. Pickett concealed a sardonic smile. But immediately after inspection and weapon training, he hurried across to the company office and carefully scrutinized the notice board. And there, on the list of potential candidates for transfer, was the name of Sergeant Jacob Rankin. Pickett gave a deep sigh of relief, though it was tinged with sadness that such a good soldier had lost his way.

The following week passed slowly for both men, who each struggled to avoid open hostility towards the other. The tension among the company of twenty-five horse soldiers was palpable. Even the most dim-witted trooper could not help but pick up on the tense atmosphere. Nothing was said, and the daily routine continued as usual. Nevertheless, both Rankin and Pickett were relieved when the officer in charge of the transfer gave notification of their departure the following morning.

\*\*\*

The flashback had been momentary. Shad Pickett quickly shook off the disquieting contemplation. So here the two former friends were, facing one another in the heart of the Pioneer Mountains some six months later. Pickett had no regrets as to how things had turned out. But what of his old associate? Was he harbouring a bitter resentment? Rankin's blank expression gave nothing away. Only when Pickett enquired about his experiences after being transferred did the deadpan look momentarily slip.

But Rankin quickly pulled himself together and outlined the bleak facts in a flat tone devoid of emotion. 'Nobody told the volunteers, especially me, that the transfer was only open to privates. That piece of news was delivered by a sadistic bastard of a sergeant once we arrived at Fort Smith. The skunk gleefully relished ordering me to remove my stripes.' A snarl of animosity now clouded Rankin's twisted face on recalling the blunt order.

Pickett couldn't contain a sly sneer, knowing as he did the upshot of the transfer. Rankin didn't notice the caustic snigger as he continued: 'Busted to the ranks I was forced to slog my guts out building a new trail right through the heart of disputed Crow tribal lands. It was back-breaking work. And every day without fail we were attacked. A good few pals were buried on that blasted highway. I was lucky to get out in one piece.'

'So what are you doing back in this part of the territory...' Pickett gave his old associate's civilian garb a suspicious appraisal '...and not in uniform?'

'After six months working on the highway to Hell, the tribes had finally been tamed and the army found that Fort Smith was overmanned. I was given the option of resigning. And I gladly accepted the offer.' A surprised look from his old superior told Rankin this was news to Pickett. 'I don't hold no grudges about what happened between us. Let the past stay there. That's what I say. And I hope you feel the same. Jake Rankin is looking to the future. So I'd deem it a great favour if'n you would drop me off at the next trading post where I can buy me a fresh horse. Then I won't bother you again.'

That was a relief to Lieutenant Pickett, who had no wish to have his old sergeant spreading idle gossip about their previous relationship at Fort Wisdom. Accordingly he was only too pleased to give the army veteran a lift to the next trading post. 'Hop on the back of the wagon,' Pickett said. 'We should be at Larapie Dan's place by this evening. You can get a fresh horse there.'

Soon after, the commander gave the order to carry on. But unbeknown to him, or the rest of the escorting contingent, they were being surreptitiously followed by five men, who kept themselves out of sight of the detail. They were under the leadership of Jake Rankin, and his presence on the trail was no accident. The shifty ex-sergeant had his devious mind set on lifting the payroll at a place of his choosing further up the trail. Meanwhile, seemingly without a care in the world, the bandit regaled Millie Denton with his daring exploits against the Crow Indians. The gullible female was left agog, much to the veiled amusement of the detail, including Pickett.

'You sure tell a good story,' the officer lightheartedly mocked his unexpected passenger. 'I'm just wondering how much of it is true.'

'You doubt my word, lieutenant?' Rankin derisively countered as his eyes flicked towards the dense mass of trees cloaking either side of the trail. His men were well hidden. 'That transfer was no easy billet, I can assure you. But the construction of the Musselshell Trail has helped prevent any future redskin uprising.'

As Pickett moved off, Rankin's whole body tensed. The site chosen for the ambush was just around the next bend.

# TWO

# HELL UNLEASHED

On rounding the sharp hairpin, the detail was forced to stop. A boulder had fallen across the narrow trail, blocking further progress. Pickett assumed that it had tumbled down from the rocky cliffs above. No suspicion of any criminal intention crossed his mind. But it would have to be moved for them to continue. 'Anders and Warrener!' he called out briskly to the two nearest troopers. 'Get this hunk of rock out the way pronto.'

As the two men put their shoulders to the task of shifting the heavy obstruction, a blast of gunfire tore apart the placid silence of the forest. One minute all was peace and tranquillity, the next birds were scattering in panic-stricken flight. The first casualty of the brutal ambush was Private Starkey. Three bullets slammed into the driver of the halted wagon, and the dead man toppled off his seat.

Although taken completely by surprise, the other troopers dropped behind the boulder, drawing their hand guns to retaliate. But their attackers were well hidden in the trees. When Anders stood to return fire he was hit in the head. It exploded like a ripe melon, a mess of bone and gristle, pitching him forwards and covering his colleague in red gore. This did nothing for Warrener's nerve as he cowered behind the boulder.

Lieutenant Pickett, who was still mounted, found himself hauled out of the saddle by a well-placed lariat. His assailant gave him no chance to recover. Leaping out from behind a rock, a young tearaway called Kid Bassett laid the barrel of his revolver across the officer's head. Pickett was knocked out cold, leaving his surviving troopers to fend for themselves.

Unable to take a clear fix on his attackers, Warrener stood little chance and was the next to go down. The bushwhackers had picked their spot well. Only Private Dupree now remained alive. Seeing his buddies all chopped down, he swung his horse around and made to escape back down the steep trail.

'Take him down with your rifle, Blacktail,' Rankin shouted. 'We don't want any of these critters queering our pitch.' The outlaw known as Blacktail Guthrie shook his long straggly hair and nodded his understanding. He carefully sighted along the barrel of the Henry repeater, then let fly with a single shot. An evil smile cracked his hard features as Dupree threw up his arms. A red splotch blossomed on the trooper's back as he disappeared from view over the edge of a ravine. Only Millie Jefferson was left alive.

The woman shrank back into the bed of the wagon, acute terror clearly emblazoned on her distraught face. 'Sorry about, this, ma'am,' Rankin apologized, pointing his gun at her. 'You weren't meant to be a part of this shindig. But we can't afford to leave any witnesses.' His gun barked once, giving Millie no chance even to scream. She sank back, eyes staring sightlessly, with a hole in her forehead. A perfect shot, if a cowardly one. Any momentary remorse for this terminal action was tempered by the avaricious glint in Rankin's eye.

While the other bushwhackers were checking that all their victims were indeed dead, the gang boss ordered Guthrie and a tall rangy jasper called Snake-eyed Rube Chiptree to haul the heavy box containing the payroll off the wagon.

Silence once again settled over the grimly forbidding landscape. Beatific solitude had been instantly transformed into a murderous killing ground. The gun battle had lasted barely five minutes, leaving four troopers dead, together with Millie Jefferson: an unfortunate casualty – wrong time, wrong place. Yet such was the way the cards of life had been dealt. Only one person had been purposely left alive: Shad Pickett had been securely tied and bundled on to his horse. Rankin had spared his life for a particular reason.

Once the iron-bound box had been loaded on to the gang's own flatbed wagon and covered with a blanket, the gang proceeded to deposit the dead troopers into the army wagon. The horses were released from their traces. They were a key element in the gang leader's plan to escape pursuit once the robbery reached the ears of the military authorities at Fort Wisdom. Its successful outcome was especially important following the brutal despatch of Millie Jefferson. Her distraught husband would be after reprisals for such a heinous crime.

The wagon was then manhandled towards the edge of the trail, where it was heaved over the rim. And there the outlaws stood in a line with Jake Rankin in the middle smiling coldly as he watched it crash down the rough slope. End over end it tumbled, smashing into rocks and small trees before finally coming to rest – an unfortunate word, to be sure – in the bed of the mountain creek below. Dust and scattered leaves enveloped what was now little more than a mangled heap of broken planks. Bits of torn clothing and exposed limbs of the brutally deceased failed to raise feelings of either guilt or remorse from the ruthless brigands.

Soldiers could expect a violent end. But no thought had been given to the poor innocent soul of Millie Jefferson, caught up in the brutal assault. A lucrative payout was all that mattered to these hard-eyed desperadoes. Rankin was about to give his final orders when he paused. A shifty-eyed cuss with prominent front choppers, appropriately named Bucktooth Axell, was tipping a bottle of hooch down his throat in celebration of the successful heist.

The gang boss grabbed the bottle out of his hand and threw it against a rock. 'There'll be no drinking until after the payout,' Rankin snarled, daring the miscreant to go for his gun. 'Get as drunk as a skunk once you've gotten your cut. But not a second before.' He then turned to address Chiptree. 'I'm putting you in charge of this detail until we meet up at the Greasy Grass hideout,' he rasped. 'All being well, that will be a week from now.' Rankin still couldn't shake off his army background and its language. 'Soon as you leave here, head straight for Saddleback where my pard Emile Lavelle will be waiting with his medicine wagon. Leave the chest with him. It'll make the perfect hideout. Nobody will suspect he's toting a stolen payroll.' He then cast a baleful eye over the listening gang members. 'And if'n I find that chest has been tampered with before the share-out in Blackfoot, some thieving critter is gonna get skinned alive.' The bizarre play on words failed to register with any of the grim-faced outlaws.

A bleak scowl was aimed at each and every man present. None chose to meet Jake Rankin's threatening stare. The boss's method of splitting up after a job before meeting for the share-out was now well established. His brusque response to indiscipline and treachery in the ranks was equally well known. Hook Nose Charlie Tapshaw had brazenly confronted their leader about his running the gang along military lines.

'So you reckon on being able to lead this detail better than me, eh Hooky?' Rankin had casually countered the blunt challenge to his authority. They were at the Greasy Grass cabin relaxing after a hard ride back from a successful heist pulled in Cascade on the banks of the Missouri when the confrontation occurred. The liquor was flowing freely, which had given Tapshaw the nerve to voice his dissent at Rankin's regimented style.

'We ain't no soldier boys,' Tapshaw's grating voice carped as he drew himself up, his absurd snout twitching as we waved a half-empty bottle of whiskey in the boss's face. 'And you treating us like squaddies on parade is a downright pain in the butt. I say you cut the high-and-mighty attitude or let a real leader take over.' The challenger's chin jutted forward. 'What do you guys say?' Silence greeted Tapshaw's suggestion. And nobody stepped forward in support.

'I suppose you're the guy who can find all these well-paying jobs and organize their execution?' Rankin casually declared, not in the least bit phased.

'Why not? I can do a sight better than you!' Tapshaw pushed his chair back, and lumbered to his feet. His presence in the gang over the last two months was essentially due to his being a slick draw artist – and not with a brush. He crouched down in the classic stance, ready to go for his gun. The others quickly moved out of the line of fire.

Rankin remained seated, a humourless smirk like a hungry sidewinder challenging the usurper to make his play. A table separated him from Hook Nose Charlie. Then he hawked out a bitter laugh.

'You ain't got the brains to run a Sunday School picnic, meathead.' The cutting jibe achieved the desired effect. Tapshaw's face turned a bright puce as he went for his gun.

His right hand had barely touched the butt when the twin blast from a hidden derringer struck him in the groin. It wasn't a killing strike, but was enough to cripple the belligerent outlaw, who went down moaning and clutching at his vitals. Rankin slowly stood up exposing the small pocket pistol he had secretly palmed beforehand. He carefully laid it down, smoke dribbling from each of the snub barrels. Then he rounded the table and stood over the stricken troublemaker.

'Just like I said, Hook Nose. You're a no-account loser,' he hissed. Slowly and with deliberation the boss drew his Navy Colt revolver, cranked back the hammer and purposefully aimed it at the gaping outlaw's head. 'And a dead one at that.' The single blast rocked the cabin, almost removing the miscreant's head in the process.

It was a brutal response to insubordination in the ranks. But it had the desired effect. Rankin casually slipped the revolver back into its holster. 'Blacktail,' he snapped out while sitting down and holding out his glass for a refill of whiskey. The outlaw was more than ready to oblige. 'Now somebody get this piece of dung outa here. He makes the place look untidy.' Immediately and without uttering a word, Kid Basset and Bucktooth Axell did as bidden. Jake Rankin had firmly and decisively established his position in no uncertain terms.

That had been three months before. And here he now stood, on a remote mountain trail having just pulled off the perfect heist. A satisfied glow softened his rough-hewn countenance at the same time, giving the impression that his hold over the gang was not all bark and bite. 'Here, catch this,' he said to Rube Chiptree, tossing the owlhoot a roll of bills. 'This caper has gone so well that I'm feeling charitable. You fellas have earned a spot of light relief. But don't spend it all in the same cat house.' A mirthful guffaw helped ease the tension that always followed a killing spree.

Snake's tongue flicked out as he hurriedly nodded his understanding. 'That's mighty generous of you, Jake.'

'Ain't it just,' the devious boss threw back, knowing full well that the dough would be deducted from their eventual payout. A final stipulation was then issued to the temporary gang leader. 'Make sure to deliver that chest to Lavelle at Saddleback. But don't hang around. And remember, no booze.' A warning gaze impaled the grouchy Axell with its sting. 'I'll meet you at Greasy Grass Gulch.'

After watching the outlaw detail make its departure for the Idaho border, Rankin secured the released horses, leading the one upon which Lieutenant Pickett was still slumped, hanging limply over the saddle horn. 'This is where I make sure you get safely back to Fort Wisdom, sucker,' Rankin muttered under his breath. 'And I'll leave the ideal trail for any pursuers to follow. This caper has put me in a good mood.' He chuckled uproariously at his ingenuity as he moved off.

The gang leader chose to make camp at Badger Pass, due to it being the highest point of the trail through the Pioneer Mountains. From there it commanded an all-round, panoramic field of vision. This was an essential element in enabling his devious scheme to proceed apace. In his avaricious mind the killer was already spending his share of the stolen money. And it was a glorious vision.

Movement of his pinioned captive brought Rankin's thoughts back to the present. When Pickett finally came round, he found himself securely tied to a tree. It felt like a blacksmith was hammering away inside his skull. He groaned, much to the delight of Jake Rankin, who was sitting on the far side of a fire drinking coffee. 'Glad to see you've finally surfaced, lieutenant,' he chuckled.

'Where am I? What happened?' the stunned officer mumbled, attempting to shake the mush from his aching head and failing miserably. That was when it all came flooding back as Rankin's smirking visage swam into focus. 'What happened to the others?' he gasped out.

'All headed for the happy hunting grounds, every last one,' the killer sniggered, enjoying the moment. 'Even Mrs Jefferson had to be sacrificed for the greater good… my good, that is. But I've saved you.' Pickett's dour response elicited another bout of guffawing. 'No need to thank me. You're going to have a lot of explaining to do about what happened up here. The next couple of days will give you the chance to figure out a good excuse for losing all that lovely dough.'

Pickett snarled, struggling ineffectually to release himself. 'You should have killed me back there, Rankin. I'll come after you, mister. Have no fear on that score.'

'Oh! I ain't afraid, soldier boy. No way,' he scoffed leaning forward. 'It's you that should be afraid when that military tribunal gets to work. Especially one chaired by that pompous clown, Colonel George Jefferson. He'll throw the book at you. If'n I was in your boots, I'd head north for Canada with me. Nobody will find us up there.' Rankin scoffed at the notion that a dedicated officer of Shad Pickett's ilk would run away from his responsibilities. 'But I reckon a mule-headed critter like you will try and play the hero and brazen it out, expecting the tribunal to see your side of things. More fool you.'

Prisoner and captor remained in the open glade high up on the trail for the next two days. Rankin was forced to gag his captive to staunch the vitriolic flow of threats. On the afternoon of the second day, he saw what he had been expecting. A patrol had been sent out from Fort Wisdom when the payroll detail had failed to arrive on schedule. They were still three hours ride down the Grasshopper valley when Rankin

27

made his move. 'I'm heading off now, lieutenant. But I'm leaving you with a horse and gun. And don't be thinking I'm doing it for some charitable motive. No, sir. You're gonna be my ticket to the good life. So don't disappoint me.'

'What makes you think I won't come after you?'

'Come after me over those mountains and you'll be accused of desertion.' Rankin had it all planned out. 'As a committed company man, that's out of the question, ain't it?' A taut silence indicated he was right. A quick look towards the plume of dust in the valley below told him the patrol was drawing ever closer. The time had come to leave this turkey for the hard-nosed carve-up of a military tribunal. He threw Pickett's gun into the bushes making sure his bonds were less than firmly tied. Another hour should see the patrol arriving. Time enough for the killer to dis-appear and Pickett to extricate himself and mount up. Stark surprise would doubtless register on both Pickett's face and that of the patrol commander when they met up.

This mug would have to think quickly to explain his being encountered many miles from the site of the robbery, not to mention being the sole survivor. Rankin smiled to himself as he pictured the outcome in his mind. Any detailed explanation from Pickett would be reserved for the tribunal. That, however, wouldn't stop the troopers discussing the gruesome episode amongst themselves. A somewhat strained atmosphere was bound to envelop the patrol on the ride back to Fort Wisdom, during which Lieutenant Pickett would be the prime object of suspicious glowers and muttered comments.

Rankin smiled to himself, confident that was how things would pan out. And he had an ace up his sleeve to ensure the blame would fall squarely on to Lieutenant Pickett's shoulders. As he waved a mocking hand of farewell to the duped officer, Jake Rankin couldn't hold back a satisfied grin that his plan of campaign was coming to fruition. Indeed it couldn't have gone down any better. The two extra mounts offered a clear indication that several riders were heading north.

# THREE

# DRUMBEAT FROM HELL

Fort Wisdom comprised little more than a cluster of wooden barracks for the enlisted men, and more salubrious two-storey accommodation for the officers. Along with stables, armoury and medical clinic, the buildings encircled a large parade ground. The military presence in the Big Hole valley was on account of a ferocious battle fought here against an Indian uprising led by Red Cloud. A small town had grown up close by. Overshadowing this alien intrusion was Odell Mountain. Even in mid-June its scalloped ramparts were coated in a layer of snow that sparkled in the sunlight.

When the search patrol arrived back at the fort, the usual drilling of troopers was being conducted. Yet even Captain Kearney, a zealot known for his fiery temper, ceased his browbeating of the men, anxious to learn the result of the expedition. Everybody in fact stopped what they were doing and stared at the dust-caked patrol. Barring none, all were eager for news of the missing payroll and its guardians. Slumped shoulders and weary looks, however, presented a grim picture that screamed out failure. And the unwholesome truth was confirmed with the absence of the payroll wagon.

Mutterings amongst the men were ignored by the officers, who were likewise stunned by this stark realization. And only one man from that much anticipated detail had returned with them. Struggling to maintain a stiff upper lip in the face of the hostile looks, Lieutenant Pickett wasted no time in reporting immediately to his commanding officer. And there in the company office he attempted to set the record straight.

But Colonel Jefferson was too distraught to listen. He needed time to reflect on the disaster that was blurted out in all its horrendous detail. He held up a hand to silence the outpouring, bluntly cutting short Pickett's explanation. 'Save anything you have to say for the court of inquiry,' the commander curtly ordered his junior officer when Pickett attempted to continue. 'That will only be conducted once the bodies of the dead troopers have been brought back and buried with full military honours in the army cemetery outside the fort.'

No mention was made of his beloved Millie. That was too much for the distraught commander to bear at that moment.

The military tribunal was not held for another three days. During that unsettling period, Shad Pickett was strongly advised to keep a low profile by moving into the town to avoid any ugly confrontations. It was a tense few days for all. When the day finally arrived for the tribunal, it was held in a separate room reserved for such issues. Only those involved in the case were present. No robbery charge was laid at Pickett's door. But being the sole survivor of the heinous massacre, a full investigation was required.

As with all such situations, a tense atmosphere hung over the courtroom gathering. Lieutenant Pickett entered the room clad in his best uniform and came to a halt in front of a raised rostrum. There he stood to attention, saluting the three senior officers handling the case, who were seated behind a long desk. Depressing and doom-laden for the main participant, it was no less sombre and grave for those handling the case, especially Colonel Jefferson.

The commander of Fort Wisdom was to deliver the tribunal's final verdict. He regarded the officer standing before him with a less than cordial reception. Indeed it was decidedly frosty in view of his grave loss, which was only to be expected. Pickett remained standing stiffly to attention while the circumstances of the inquiry were read out by an orderly. 'Do you have any representation to conduct your case?' asked Major Freemont, a member of the tribunal, maintaining a critical manner as befitted the seriousness of the investigation.

'No sir,' Pickett replied, with an assured poise, holding the other officer's intent frown. 'I will be conducting my own defence, and have every confidence that the tribunal will exonerate me from any blame for this most heinous of crimes.'

'Do you have any objection to Captain Kearney conducting the inquiry on behalf of the military authorities?' the commanding officer asked.

'No sir,' was Pickett's stilted reply, even though he was aware that Kearney was noted for being particularly forceful in his cross-examinations of witnesses at disciplinary hearings such as this. A shuffling of papers by the panel was followed by whispered asides between the three members before the hearing proper began. The formal swearing-in oath was then taken, with the officer under investigation holding a bible.

Thereafter Lieutenant Pickett was allowed to give his version of events. Being the only survivor of the attack, everything depended on how he conducted himself in persuading these grim-faced officers that he had stood no chance against such a brutal ambush. It was a heart-felt and impassioned explanation. That said, it lacked specific detail due to Pickett having been knocked unconscious at the very start of the attack. His whole case depended on convincing the panel that ex-sergeant Jake Rankin was the perpetrator.

'He tried persuading me that he was heading north,' Pickett insisted with vigour at the end of his grilling by Kearney. Under the circumstances, he was satisfied with the way things had gone. 'The skunk had even commandeered some loose horses to provide a clear trail for any pursuing patrol to follow. But that was merely a false lead.' He shook his head dismissing this explanation. 'My theory is that he intended pushing south to where the rest of his gang were waiting to divide up their ill-gotten gains.'

Kearney chose that moment to interrupt the ardent vindication. 'So what you are saying, Lieutenant Pickett, is that your entire justification for fleeing the scene of this awful attack…'

An incensed Shad Pickett butted in to deny his accuser's claim: 'I did not run away, sir. I only came to my senses when Rankin left me at Badger Pass.'

'That is your claim. But please tell the court if I am wrong…' Kearney paused as he strutted around, secure in the knowledge he had this culpable officer over a barrel '…What you are saying is that ex-sergeant Jacob Rankin is the leader of this alleged gang of thieves…'

'That is right. Rankin is the guilty party here, not me!' Pickett's voice had risen, as anger threatened to disrupt his unruffled composure.

A leery smirk greeted this assertion as Kearney continued: '…and that he, for some unaccountable reason, permitted you to live…?' Another poignant pause followed, while the officer caustically emphasized his query by stabbing a finger at the object of his accusation. At the same time he aimed a cynical look towards the panel '...to then be discovered free as a bird by the searching patrol sent out when your detail failed to arrive here. Are you asking the tribunal to believe such a cock-and-bull story?'

Kearney's chin was thrust forwards as he awaited the explanation.

'It's true,' Pickett shouted, though immediately regretted his outburst. 'He wanted me to take the blame for the robbery. But it's Rankin who should be standing here now, not me. And if'n the tribunal permits, I want to lead a patrol in search of the killer and recover the stolen money. As I said before, my theory is that he made us all think he was heading north for Canada. But it's my belief it was a trick and he is really going south.'

Pickett held his breath while looking at the panel for their reaction to his earnest allegation. And for the first time, it appeared that they were coming round to accepting his viewpoint. Various positive nods and whispered remarks passed between them. That was the moment Captain Kearney chose to make a revelation he had thus far kept secret: allow an opponent to think he was home and dry before dropping the bolt from the blue. 'All of your testimony hangs on Rankin being the culprit. Please confirm that avowal to the panel.' His manner was delivered in a reserved, innocuous manner.

'That is what I am asserting. Yes.'

The interrogator then passed Pickett a picture for him to identify. 'Would you agree that this is trooper Jacob Rankin?'

'That's him all right. No doubt in my mind,' Pickett declared, falling right into Kearney's trap as the officer produced a sheet of parchment which he handed to Colonel Jefferson. 'This is an official copy, sir, taken from army records, which states that the said soldier, then Private Jacob Rankin, was killed in action while helping to defend a newly laid road against a marauding band of Crow Indians.' The gloating prosecutor fastened a beady eye on to the accused, whose ashen face betrayed his shock at this surprise announcement. 'In view of this damning evidence, Lieutenant Pickett, how do you explain Rankin's involvement in this murderous event?'

'B-but it c-can't b-be true,' Pickett stammered out, unable to comprehend what was being asserted. 'It was him and his gang who carried out the raid.'

Kearney ignored the denial. 'You thought to pass the blame for this robbery on to a dead man to conceal your own failings when you fled the scene of the attack, leaving brave soldiers and a proud woman to be decimated. There is only one word to describe such a spineless officer...' He pointed a damning finger at the stunned officer, who was lost for words. 'You, sir, are a blatant coward. I rest my case.' He then sat down.

A profound silence, heavy with foreboding, laid its icy hand across the sombre proceedings. The revelation had stunned them all, and none more so than Shad Pickett. The stark realization that Jake Rankin had well and truly cooked his goose, gripped the hoodwinked victim in a tight embrace he could not shake off. No wonder the skunk had been so all-fired certain he could get away with this awful crime. Somehow he had managed to switch identities with a dead soldier. That was the only explanation possible.

'Has the accused anything to say regarding this charge?' the clerk of the tribunal declared in a sombre tone.

Shad looked at the strait-laced, dour faces of the panel. Convincing them that such a theory held water would be like swimming against a strong current. It was as clear as a new moon that they were convinced *he* was the guilty party, and not the allegedly deceased perpetrator. Any attempt to deny that he had lied to the court would be ignored. All he could do was shake his head.

Colonel Jefferson then addressed the small gathering. 'This tribunal has listened to the findings and will now retire to consider its response. The accused will remain here until such time as a verdict has been reached.'

'All stand in court,' the clerk's sober voice boomed out. Two guards standing at the rear immediately moved forwards to stand behind where Shad Pickett was standing. The powers that be were giving him no chance to abscond. All he could do now was reflect on the trap he had fallen into and its grim consequences.

Outside, the general noise of an army fort going about its daily routine carried on, unaffected by the changes about to be wrought on the life of Lieutenant Shadrak Pickett. The panel were out for no more than ten minutes. It was a clear-cut case that required little discussion, apart from the sentence to be imposed. When the tribunal resumed, Pickett was ordered to stand to attention before the panel.

As expected, no look of sympathy was evident on any of the three hard-faced officers. Colonel Jefferson cleared his throat. His voice wavered with emotion as he announced the panel's unanimous verdict. 'Of the charges brought before this tribunal, we have no proof that you, Lieutenant Pickett, had any involvement in the robbery and murder that took place on the mountain road. Although serious questions still need to be answered as to why you attempted to place the blame on a dead soldier.'

'But he isn't dead, sir. I was…'

'The accused will be silent while the colonel is stating the panel's findings,' Captain Kearney's testy interruption effectively curtailed Pickett's heated intervention. He could only hope that the panel's verdict would not be too damning.

Colonel Jefferson aimed a caustic look in Pickett's direction before continuing. There was no mercy evident in his pitiless gaze. 'Our only conclusion is that you panicked when the first shots were fired and then fled the scene…' The colonel's voice faltered. He swallowed down the anguish threatening to overwhelm him before continuing, '…leaving others to suffer the consequences.

'You then concocted this blatant lie to cover your own shortcomings. Accordingly we have no choice but to regard your heinous action as a gross dereliction of duty. For this unseemly act of craven cowardice there can only be one sentence.' The colonel paused to draw breath before continuing with his denunciation. 'Had you been an enlisted man, it would have been a firing squad. As it is I am only allowed to pass a dishonourable discharge from the service. But be under no illusions. That will be written up and distributed to every news agency throughout the surrounding territories.'

All colour drained from the accused man's face. How had it come to this? One day a highly respected officer, the next reduced to a lily-livered chicken. Shad Pickett couldn't feel any more wretched. His legs felt like jelly. Grabbing hold of a chair to maintain an upright bearing he struggled to preserve some form of dignity.

'Do you have anything more to say before the sentence is carried out?'

Pickett was breathing hard. His heart was pumping like a steam engine inside his chest. Cowardice! There was no more despicable label with which a man could be tarred. And all on account of that conniving dog Jake Rankin. A glint of hate at what this man had done overshadowed any feeling of self-pity. 'I would deem it a favour if the court could give me Rankin's picture,' he said trying to maintain an even temper. 'All I want to do is clear my name by bringing this skunk to justice.'

No objections were voiced as the picture was handed over. Colonel Jefferson stood up. 'This court of inquiry is adjourned. Take this man away. I do not want to see him ever again.' Two waiting guards immediately stepped forwards and frog-marched the accused out of the room. Outside were ranged the majority of Fort Wisdom's garrison. Bad news of this nature travels faster than the desert wind, and every single man wanted to witness a ritual most of them had never experienced before.

A low murmur speckled with epithets rippled through the ranks as the object of their scorn was led out on to the open parade ground. Some of the comments expressed were sympathetic to the victim. 'Who would have thought that a respected officer like Pickett would have shirked his duty,' one old soldier remarked scratching his bald head. 'A skunk that lets other men die by running off deserves all he's gonna get.' That was the majority view as the muttering swelled to a menacing growl.

The angry tumult subsided when Captain Kearney stepped forwards, declaring in a loud voice: 'Private Isaac, step forwards and do your duty.' The trooper in question had been quickly briefed as to the procedure to be followed. It was the ultimate degradation to have a lowly enlisted man carry out the humiliating ritual laid down for the crime of cowardice.

A slow hand-clap began as a nervous Jubal Isaac faced the convicted officer. He could not look the disgraced man in the eye as he ripped the twin-pipped epaulettes from both shoulders. The buttons on his tunic followed them into the dust. With each shiny brass disc torn from its fastening Shad Pickett felt as if his whole being was being pulled apart.

The final humiliation was the removal of the sword from its scabbard. The crisp snap echoed across the parade ground as the blade was cracked in half across the poor trooper's knee. The young soldier's sweat-bathed features almost made Shad feel sorry for him. Glad the ugly task was completed, Isaac hurriedly stepped away, relieved to lose himself amidst the surging crowd of troopers.

The harsh procedure completed, Pickett's horse was led forwards. The saddlebags had been hastily filled with all his worldly goods. There wasn't much to show for ten years' faithful service. Immediately eight drummers began beating out the haunting rhythm normally reserved for funerals. On this occasion it conveyed no essence of bereavement: this was the devil's tune, a fitting culmination to a shamed officer's career. It was the final nail in the coffin for a man now unjustly reduced to a nomadic pariah, condemned to wander alone and shunned by all.

As Pickett mounted up and headed for the outer cordon of the fort, the growl of anger rose to a bare-faced expression of the men's feelings towards such a craven lowlife. None of the officers present made any attempt to quell the raucous clamour. And as if in accord with the ugly mood enveloping Fort Wisdom, dark clouds that had been gathering opened their doors. The flash storm that followed did, however, effectively douse the hostile atmosphere as men ran for cover.

Only Shad Pickett remained unaffected by the drenching. Plodding onward in a daze, he quickly, and gratefully, disappeared into the murky wall of falling water.

# FOUR

## SOUTHBOUND

The shamed ex-lieutenant's first objective was to examine the wreckage of the doomed payroll wagon. Perhaps he could pick up some clue as to which direction the robbers had taken. Retracing his journey of the previous week was a grim undertaking, and as he drew closer to the macabre site, he began to wonder if he would ever find Rankin and bring him back to clear his name. His head hung low at the bleak prospect facing him.

This was only a brief moment of despair, however, as he knew that fleeing the territory to start afresh offered no answer. Even some remote place where the name of Shad Pickett was unknown would still leave the yellow label of coward dogging him wherever he went. The only answer was to track Rankin down and force a confession from the varmint's lips, no matter how long it took. Only his 'resurrection' under arrest would wipe the slate clean.

Then suddenly, there it was: a heap of mangled wreckage still lying in the bottom of the ravine. All the details he had learned regarding the terrible event had come from Rankin's poisonous mouth. And that was precious little. Slowly and with much trepidation he dismounted and made his way down through the tangle of broken trees and shrubbery to the bleak site of destruction. At least there was no sign of the human carnage wrought here. The recovery detachment had done their job well – and examination of the ghastly locale unfortunately revealed nothing of value to aid his quest for retribution.

With a shrug of despondency he turned around to retrace his steps. And that was when he noticed a plume of smoke drifting in the still air some fifty yards upstream from the wreck. Immediately alert that maybe the killers had returned, perhaps figuring to ransack the dead bodies, he dodged behind a tree, gun drawn and ready. Nothing moved. It appeared that the smoke was coming from a camp fire. Silently and with great care he approached the site. A man was seated on a log with his back to the avenger.

'One false move, mister, and you're a dead man,' he growled out, making his presence known. The man stiffened, raising his hands. 'What are you doing sniffing around here? Come back to gloat, have you?'

'I was just passing by and noticed the wreckage of that wagon,' the man asserted nervously. 'Didn't mean no harm. All I wanted was some spare wood to make a fire.' He pointed to the makings – a black frying pan and even blacker coffee pot, steam billowing from its spout. 'I can offer you a cup if'n you'll just put that gun away.' The guy was an old-timer and clearly posed no threat, so Shad did as he asked. A burro grazing nearby loaded with mining gear indicated that the fella was a prospector. 'The name's Rockerbox Riley.'

The colourful handle told Shad his assumption had been right. He stepped forward to accept the proffered cup. 'Much obliged, Rocker, don't mind if'n I do.'

That was when Riley noticed the shabby uniform. 'Soldier boy, eh?' he muttered attempting a toothy smile. 'I did my bit for the union…' The words congealed in his mouth and the affable smile disappeared, replaced by a chary eye as it passed over the torn shoulder tabs. That was when the penny dropped.

His old head nodded, the lower lip curling with abhorrence. 'I heard about you. You're that Shad Pickett, ain't yuh?' He didn't wait for a reply. The coffee cup was upended, its contents splashing the accused man's boots. 'You ain't welcome here, yellow jacket. Best be on your way.' The candid indictment was detached, icy in its lack of empathy. Neither did any fear regarding the insult register in the old prospector's stark gaze.

No response was forthcoming. The blunt accusation had left the wronged man totally shaken. The proverb that bad news travelled fast was no idle premise. All he could do was dolefully turn away and leave. Now he understood exactly what it felt like to be an outsider, an outcast, a leper wandering in purgatory. The need to find Jake Rankin and hopefully the stolen payroll was now firmly embedded in his consciousness. All he could think of was wringing a confession from the bastard's foul lips. Until that was achieved, he would be condemned to living in the shadows.

He could not get away from the chilling location of his ignominy fast enough, and left at a gallop. His horse would have paid the price of the panic-induced departure had not Shad's army training as a cavalry officer stepped in to prevent a disaster. 'Always treat a horse like one of the family and it will respond accordingly.' Much as he wanted to press onwards, he forced himself to rest the lathered beast, thereafter slowing his pace to a steady trot. Being cast afoot in this wild outback would be fatal.

The only suitable place to leave the mountain road was by means of the ferry over Elkhorn Creek. Bannock's Crossing was reached later that day. It was little more than a cluster of shacks that offered meagre sustenance to tired travellers while they awaited passage across the creek. The ferry was a flimsy-looking conveyance, no more than a line of pine logs lashed together and surrounded by roped uprights, which offered scant protection for horse and rider. Cables supported on each side of creek were attached to a windlass anchored at one end of the ferry. It provided the sole means of propulsion.

'You sure have been pushing that cayuse mighty hard, mister,' the ferryman remarked, noting the white lather caking the animal's flanks. 'Something spooked you up there?' The grizzled veteran slung a thumb towards the towering bulk of the Pioneers.

Pickett had to think of an excuse quickly as he led the horse on to the rickety structure. The unwelcome query as to his haste was made even more tricky when he spotted a copy of the *Montana Gazette* sticking out of the jigger's pocket. Surely there hadn't been time for the bizarre events at Fort Wisdom to have been included in the latest edition.

'Thought I spotted some Indians a while back,' he replied. 'Can't trust those critters one jot.' He then diverted the ferryman's attention by asking him for a look at the paper.

The man handed it over, apparently satisfied with the excuse. 'Don't look so worried,' he gently chided his client. 'I ain't never lost a passenger yet. Although there's always a first time. Maybe you'll be the unlucky one!' A raucous guffaw followed the witty aside as the man focused his whole attention on the ferry winding cable.

Shad did not share his pilot's blasé manner. Far from it. But what other choice did he have? It was either this or a substantial detour. An enquiry from the ferryman had revealed that the next crossing point was two days downstream. He could not afford

47

to waste that kind of time if his quest was to bear fruit. All he could do was hunker down while a jaundiced eyebrow flicked through the news sheet. Thankfully it revealed nothing to bother him. Care to avoid being recognized would doubtless come later. Nevertheless it was with some relief that he returned the paper.

Too late now to change his mind, anyway. The ferry had left the jetty behind. This was the narrowest point, and the creek was in full spate. Galloping white horses raced each other, jostling for position to negotiate the fermenting narrows. It was like the Kentucky Derby. In amongst the foaming rapids were tree trunks dislodged from further up in the mountain fastness. Their sole aim in the fearful mind of the lone passenger was to tear the small craft from its fixing stanchions

After what seemed like a full beard's growth of time – though in effect it was little more than fifteen minutes – the ferry bumped up against the jetty on the far side. Never was a passenger more relieved to set foot on dry land. 'What's the nearest town from here?' he asked the old-timer, anxious to divest himself of the desecrated blue uniform.

'Head south over the divide yonder and you should hit Saddleback in two days,' was the man's direct reply.

Pickett's next question was posed in a diffident tone of voice so as not to appear too over eager. Just a casual enquiry. 'You get many travellers through here?' he asked, getting ready to mount up.

'Some,' was the offhand reply. 'A bit lean recently, though. Maybe it's on account of them redskins you spotted. Last fella was four days ago. He was also heading south.' Much as he wanted to press the issue, Pickett made no further comment. Thankfully the ferryman confirmed his suspicions that this was Jake Rankin. 'He had a scar on his left cheek. It looked to me like a knife wound. Tall, rangy guy, and in a hurry, too. He couldn't get away fast enough when we landed.'

That was Rankin all right. If nothing else the scar was a definite pointer. Shad could even remember how his old associate had acquired it. The occasion was emblazoned on his subconscious. It was during that notable skirmish on Lodge Tail Ridge. One of Little Wolf's braves had launched himself at the officer, and only the quick-witted response from Corporal Rankin had saved him from certain death. The trooper had received that knife wound for his heroic rescue. And Second Lieutenant Pickett had ensured he had been made up to sergeant as a result.

Now here he was, hunting the guy down. How was it possible for one man to change so dramatically from being a brave, stalwart trooper into a cold-blooded killer? It was beyond his comprehension. But Rankin had dealt the cards from a stacked deck and would have to pay the price. The avenger was now certain he was on the right trail to achieve that end. However, just to make certain he had the right man, he slowly withdrew the photograph and showed it to the ferryman. 'That him?' he said, forcing the nervous inflection from his voice.

The old guy perused the picture carefully before replying: 'That's him all right,' he averred, fastening a curious eye on his passenger. 'You gotten a beef with this guy?'

This time Shad was ready with a suitable answer. 'He owes me big time. Ran out on a poker game after giving me an IOU. I aim to collect, in full.' He didn't elaborate on how he aimed to collect.

\*\*\*

Crossing the divide entailed following an old Indian track that snaked up and up into ever bleaker terrain. It was a cold business, with snow becoming deeper on the ground as height was gained. Shad was mighty glad to have his army greatcoat available. Thankfully the key to a safe passage through the mountains was by way of a narrow gap called Clark's Elbow. It was an unusual split in the rock wall that bent at a sharp angle mid-way along. And there, clearly imprinted in a patch of snow, he came across a single set of hoofprints.

As the track descended and the snow melted on the far side of the divide, Shad lost the trail. It disappeared entirely on the marshy grassland below where the valley of the Salmon River split into three separate tributaries. The ferryman had told him to look out for a headland distinguished by twin buttes of rock known as the Two Gossips, and to take the left-hand watercourse. This decision found him entering the small town of Saddleback later that day.

A weary-looking berg on a bend of the Lemni River, Saddleback had grown up where a bridge spanned the gently flowing waters. The shadows of a drab dusk did nothing to enhance the allure of the place. But at least it had a general store where Shad was able to buy some much needed civilian clothes – the sooner he ditched his army duds the better. A feisty young girl served him. And it was made blatantly obvious from her come-hither look that more than just mercantile goods could be his for the taking. It would appear that Saddleback had a marked dearth of eligible young men.

Unbeknown to the girl, her sassy behaviour had been spotted by a protective brother, who now brusquely made his presence known. 'Get yourself up to your room straightaway,' the older man snapped, fixing his sister with a sternly disapproving stare. 'I'll see to this gentleman.'

Fear registered on the girl's face. 'I weren't doing nothing wrong, Ike,' she protested, trying to distance herself from any immodest intentions. 'Just wanted to be friendly, is all.'

Ike Sheridan was having none of it. Neither was the customer, who immediately stood back, not wanting to become entangled in any family dispute. 'I told you to go,' the man growled, his tone noticeably harden-ing. 'You're nought but a brazen hussy. Now do like I say.' Eve Sheridan was about to voice a spirited rebut-tal of this accusation, but thought better of it. Giving a pert shrug of the shoulders, she spun around and stalked off.

Once his sister had departed, Ike Sheridan turned to address the newcomer. 'Sorry about that, mister. Eve ain't yet learned how to behave properly among strangers.'

'None of my business,' Shad declared. 'All I came in for was to buy these duds.' He laid down a pair of levis, a green check shirt and tan leather vest, along with a new high-crown Stetson. After paying for the goods he asked: 'Is there some place I could change?' The proprietor directed him to a room at the back. Ten minutes later, Shad emerged a different man. He placed his old clothes on the counter. 'I'd be obliged if'n you'd burn these.'

Sheridan glanced at them. It was obvious that they were army apparel, but he made no comment. It was clear to the customer that this guy also had no inkling as to his identity. So with a measure of relief he left the store. But only to circle around to the rear where the girl had gone. A light was shining in a room that he guessed must be Eve Sheridan's quarters. The intensely hard set now gracing his features certainly did not hint of any carnal purpose.

A light tap on the door was followed seconds later by a sensuous whisper, 'Come in, honey. The door ain't locked.' And there stood Eve, affecting what she believed was her most alluring pose, all her womanly features on display. She sidled up to this handsome stranger. 'I figured it would be you. We don't get many handsome visitors to Saddleback since the mine went bust.' The fingers of her left hand etched a trail up Shad's vest.

But if she was expecting a lustful response, Eve Sheridan was to be disappointed. Shad pushed her away. His ardent gaze was not fastened on a heaving breast, but on the brooch pinned to her blouse. He grabbed it, tearing the material and eliciting a fearful cry from the girl. 'Where did you get this?' he snarled, gripping her arm tightly.

Eve pulled away. 'What's that to you?' she shot back, now knowing she had badly misjudged the stranger's visit. 'It's mine. I bought it from a passing salesman.'

'Don't lie to me,' Shad persisted, his voice rising, his eyes full of rancour. 'Now tell me, who gave it to you?'

The girl could not ignore the brutal lines of hate written large across this man's craggy face as he waved the brooch in her face. Fear for her own safety returned. 'All right, all right, I'll tell you. A man called here a few days ago and gave it to me...'

'Was he alone? Where had he come from?' The questions were punched out with vigour as Shad roughly grabbed her arm. 'Come on, tell me!'

'He wanted to buy a fresh horse, but Ike told him we didn't have any for sale. So he left after...' She left the obvious attraction other than a fresh horse hanging in the air.

'What did he look like? Where was he headed?' Shad's face was alight with expectation as the questions came out as if from a rampant gatling gun.

'I don't know nothing, mister. All I can tell you is that he was a tall fella with a scar on his left cheek.' A smile that failed to reach his eyes cracked Shad Pickett's grim countenance. It had to be Rankin. To confirm his assumption he showed her the picture. 'Is that him?' It took a deal of frowning before she slowly nodded. 'Although he sure didn't look that smart. When he left he headed south.'

South. Still heading south. 'What's the next town in that direction?' Shad rapped out. Eager now to get rid of this frightening intruder, Eve blurted out. 'It's the border town of Bitterroot. Three days ride from here on the Snake Flats.'

Shad nodded. But just as he turned away to leave, the door opened. And there stood Ike Sheridan, red of face with fists bunched. 'I figured after that last skunk came here this would happen,' he growled out grabbing the girl and raising a hand.

'It weren't like that, Ike,' Eve cried out cowering away. 'He'd just lost his way.'

The storekeeper hawked out a cynical laugh as he made to strike the girl. Shad managed to grip his arm pushing him away. No way was he about let this burly critter beat the girl on his account. 'She's telling the truth,' he said standing over the incensed man.

But Ike was not listening. He snarled out a lurid epithet as he scrambled to his feet and launched himself at what he mistakenly believed was a besmirching of his sister's reputation. But intense anger had blurred his actions and Shad easily side-stepped the haymaking swing. A single blow, sharply delivered to the passing exposed chin effectively terminated the one-sided contest. Ike Sheridan went down in a heap and stayed there.

Shad made for the door eager to get away. 'Hang on, mister,' Eve called out before he could leave. Her face registered a woebegone look as she held out a hand. 'You don't want that brooch, do you?' For the first time since he had arrived in Saddleback, Shad's face registered a sympathetic smile. His eyes dropped to the jewel in his hand. It was probably the only present the girl had ever been given. 'Guess not,' he answered, placing it gently into her hand.

'Gee thanks, mister. I appreciate that…and good luck with your quest.'

'But just remember, whenever you pin it on,' the enigmatic stranger cautioned, 'it was stolen from a dead woman.' Eve gulped. This blunt revelation was as unexpected as the receipt of the gift. 'And say a prayer that I'm able to bring her killer to justice.'

Another smile, and her mysterious benefactor was swallowed up by the night… heading south. At least he was travelling in the right direction. Sooner or later he would run the skunk to ground. And then there would be hell to pay. Pickett's version.

Keeping to a general southerly course, Shad called on various horse traders hoping to track down his quarry. But none had recently sold a horse to the man in the photograph or sporting a scar on his left cheek. Sometime later a sign told him that he was now entering the territory of Idaho. Maybe his luck would change here.

# FIVE

# NO HIDING PLACE

Up ahead he could see a cluster of buildings that must be the town of Bitterroot. It was sited where four trails crossed in the middle of the Snake River Plains. And judging by the bustling main street, it had a sight more going for it than Saddleback.

Shad was tired out and badly in need of a bed for the night. The Occidental Hotel offered the ideal sleepover. But first he needed a drink and some information. He drew up at the first saloon, boasting the appropriate name of The Rattler's Kiss. Tying off at the hitch rail, he unfastened his saddle bag and stepped up on to the boardwalk. The inside of the saloon was like a hundred others he had visited, a long mahogany bar on his left with numerous green baize tables scattered about where gamblers were plying their trade.

Smoke from numerous tallow lamps blended with that from a myriad cigars. At one end of the saloon, perched on a small stage, sat a three-piece band belting out a well known ditty. The jarring din added to the boisterous cacophony. Shad elbowed his way over to the bar and ordered a beer. Painted on the back mirror was the usual scantily clad doxy. But this one had a snake draped around her body, its lascivious tongue flicking at her cheek.

The barman sidled up, noticing his interest in the picture. 'This place used to be called The Lady's Kiss,' he explained while pouring out a beer for his customer. 'But I've had too many bad experiences with false-hearted women so I had that snake added. It makes fellas think twice before committing themselves.' He hawked out a cynical guffaw. 'What do you reckon, stranger?'

'It sure is a unique way of looking at the opposite sex, I'll give you that,' Shad commented. 'But I'm more interested in finding this jasper.' He removed the photograph from his pocket and laid it on the bar top. 'Has he passed through Bitterroot?'

The barman eyed the print, his rotund features creasing in thought. 'Can't say I've seen him around here,' he said pushing it along the bar. 'How about you fellas?'

The man standing next to Shad nodded his head. 'Yep, I saw this fella,' he confirmed. 'Only a couple of days back. I own the livery stable and I sold him a fresh horse. His own was done in, ready for the knacker's yard.'

Shad's eyes lit up. 'What kind of horse did he buy?'

'It was a brown and white paint,' the ostler replied.

That was the moment his pal butted in snatching up the print. A puzzled frown cracked his bearded face. 'That's Jake Rankin. My brother was with the same outfit based at Fort Wisdom in Montana. I'm Buck Anders.' The man was clearly nonplussed by what he was seeing. Even more so when the questioner's face assumed a shocked expression. 'Poor guy was killed in an ambush led by a yellow-bellied officer called Pickett,' Anders continued, scrutinizing Shad with wary suspicion. 'So what business do you have with this guy, mister?' That was the moment his eyes widened.

'You know this guy, Buck?' his pal enquired.

'You're darned tooting I do. You're Pickett, ain't you?' he shouted, his voice rising above the general hubbub. 'I saw you at Fort Wisdom once when I was visiting Buck. There's a pen drawing of your ugly mug in this week's *Idaho Guardian*.' Anders raised his hands calling out for quiet. His urgent insistence effectively stifled the clamour as men eagerly turned to see what all the disturbance was about. Now that he had the whole saloon listening in, the speaker voiced his accusation in no uncertain terms.

He jabbed a finger at the object of his derision. 'The paper has a damning report of how this skunk ran away and left his men to get massacred by a bunch of robbers who took the army payroll. He was drummed out of the service for cowardice, laying the blame on a dead soldier.' He lifted the photo into the air for all to see before continuing his diatribe. 'My brother was killed in the line of duty while this critter goes free. And here he is, drinking in our saloon large as life. What do you reckon we should do to a guy what does that, boys?'

Too much hard liquor and Anders' ardent indictment were enough to turn a group of happy carousing drinkers into a blood-crazed mob. 'String him up!' The frenzied submission was fervently taken up by the rest. 'Yeh, hang the yeller bastard!' A rope had suddenly appeared and was being fashioned into a noose.

Shad knew that if he was to get out of there without having his neck stretched, immediate action was needed. Luckily for him he was at the end of the bar close to a door. As the crowd surged forwards to grab hold of their victim, Shad drew back, the army Remington gripped tightly in his right hand. A couple of bullets were aimed at one of the tallow lamps hanging from the ceiling. It shattered into a thousand pieces, the burning oil splashing over nearby tables, setting the green felt ablaze. That certainly cooled the crowd's courage, turning the grizzly situation his way as men strove to avoid the flaming cascade.

A cry of horror arose from the barman's lips as the fire quickly took hold. The deafening roar of the six-gun and its aftermath was successful in halting the mob's advance. But Shad knew it was only temporary. Their blood was up, and in that state of agitation nothing would stop them from achieving their gruesome goal.

He quickly backed towards the door. The gun jabbed at the howling throng. Another bullet chewed wood fragments from a ceiling support as he prayed the door was unlocked. Providence was on his side. The door swung open, and he was through. Bolting it from the inside, he was just in time as the first shoulder slammed into the far side. But how long would it hold up against a surging mass of powerful, angry men?

Shad did not wait to find out. He dashed over to the far side and out of another door that gave on to a back alley. Nobody was about. The commotion at the front, however, indicated that some of the more astute patrons were attempting to cut off his escape. His horse would have to be abandoned. He hustled off along a rear passage, desperately searching for a fresh one. Two blocks down he came upon the livery stable.

A quick peek inside told him it was empty. The other ostlers must have abandoned their responsibilities to investigate the furore down the street. Two horses were ready saddled. Shad chose a fine-looking appaloosa, giving thanks to his Maker that he had taken his goods along into the saloon. He led the horse outside and mounted up.

Before leaving he stuck a twenty dollar bill on the other mount's saddle. Shad Pickett was no coward, but neither did he want to be labelled a horse thief.

The main street was out of the question, so he wove a tortuous course between numerous back lots and shacks to emerge on the south side of the town.

The rowdy discord brought a leery half smile to the fugitive's flushed countenance. That sure was a close call, but he had made good his escape, and hopefully the fire would keep them busy for a spell. Time now to stir the dust. The appaloosa did not disappoint as its long legs stretched out, eating up the miles. Only when Shad was satisfied he was not being followed did he bring the animal down to a steady canter. The mood of relief at having avoided a lingering death was tempered by the dismal knowledge that every man's hand was now against him.

It certainly hadn't taken long for the unsettling news of his debasement to spread across the country like a rampant outbreak of cholera. From here on he could not ignore the fact that he was most definitely a man alone.

A stoical look took in the distant horizon, where grey clouds swirled around high mountain peaks on the far side of the Snake River plain. As far as the eye could see in all directions, his was the only human presence. It was a comforting notion, whilst at the same time it brought home the stark truth of his isolation, in all sense of the meaning.

He pushed on towards the mountains, entering a remote landscape of rocky crags interspersed with dense pine forests. Had he known that these valleys were drained by the Lost River and its tributaries, he could have sympathized with the name. But all he could do was continue south, trusting that eventually he would strike lucky. After four days of accompanying the Big Lost, he dropped down into a wide enclosed valley. A sign nailed to a tree pointed south of east to a place called Arco Butte.

He slowed the appaloosa to a walk as he neared the lonely enclave that comprised little more than a general store, the obligatory saloon and various other buildings. A long blink and you would be out the other side. Would anybody in this secluded faraway locale have heard of the name Shad Pickett? He doubted it. More important though, had Jake Rankin passed through here?

That question was answered when he spotted the lone horse tied outside the saloon. It was a brown and white paint. His whole body stiffened. There were plenty of other horses with the same colouring, yet it seemed too much of a coincidence that this one was on his route south. Caution dogged his every move as he approached the single-storey building. Eyes fixed on the entrance, he dismounted and drew his gun.

# SIX

# CHALLENGE

Cracks and bangs from around the side of the saloon saw him crouching low. The question flashed in his head: had he been spotted first, with Rankin laying another ambush? Moments passed with no further shooting, so he peered around the saloon corner, only to see a few local kids setting off firecrackers. Relief was soon etched starkly across his pinched features –and then he remembered: it was the 4th July – Independence Day. Inside the saloon, nobody else was taking any notice of the outdoor racket.

Shad edged his way into the shadowy interior allowing his eyes to adjust to the gloom before making his presence felt. And there stood his quarry, facing away and totally unaware that he was under observation. Rankin was about to refill his glass from a whiskey bottle on the bar. 'You won't be needing that drink where you're headed, Jake.' The sudden and unexpected intrusion caught Rankin off guard. He froze, the bottle half way to the glass. 'Put it down slow and easy. Last thing I want is to tote a corpse back to Fort Wisdom.'

Rankin did as ordered before slowly turning to face his nemesis. 'You've gotten more gumption than I gave you credit for, lieutenant.' The snigger that followed made Shad grit his teeth. No way was he gonna let this critter get under his skin. 'Sorry about that. I should have said *Mister* Pickett seeing as you've been drummed out of the service for cowardice.' A derisive guffaw found the victim of the mordant humour itching to pull the trigger. But Rankin knew that to do so would not help him to regain his damaged status. He then addressed the barman. 'This greenhorn patsy took the rap for my misdemeanour.' More laughter. 'And now he thinks I'll stand by and let him take me back. More fool you, buster.'

The barman was all ears to see how this fracas would pan out. A convicted coward and the guy that framed him. All happening here in his saloon. It was the best action they'd had in Arco Butte since King High Johnny Dymond took the Eureka Gold Mine off that swell-headed Franz Pumpernickel. The high-stakes poker game on that day had been an all-nighter. And what a moment for this present heave-ho to happen. Independence Day. The kids were already celebrating outside.

But Pastor Skoot Amory had no wish for his establishment to take a licking should his current customer decide to resist, as he was sure he would. The saloon owner ascertained that the double-barrelled sawn-off shotgun was close to hand should it be required. Being a pastor he also acted as the religious conscience of the tiny community, transforming his premises into a House of God on a Sunday. The observant drinker could not avoid heeding this unusual extra function, with a large bible resting in a central position behind the bar. That effectively meant that there was no alcoholic consumption on the Lord's Day. At least not in the saloon.

However, the self-appointed minister was no prude. Today was Tuesday. So normal service, inclusive of gambling, was permitted. Nor did he hold back when the need for strong language dictated. 'You guys want to kick the shit out of each other, it's okay with me. But I'd be obliged if'n you'd do it in the street. Then all the town can enjoy the fun.'

'There won't be no trouble, pop,' Shad casually replied keeping a sharp eye on his adversary. 'That is, if'n *Mister* Rankin here don't wanna end up strapped across the saddle. Not a very comfortable way to travel.' Then for the listener's benefit, added with a contemptuous inflection, 'He's right, though. Me being tarred with a yellow streak is all thanks to this treacherous rat. So I have every intention of taking you back, Rankin. You're gonna admit before that tribunal what really happened that day. And just to make sure I'm exonerated, it'll be written down on paper.'

'I ain't gonna sign no confession,' Rankin blurted out, scoffing as he added with a smirk, 'You know as well as me that I never had the learning to do that.' A disgruntled grunt accompanied the uncomfortable admission.

Shad laughed out loud, a malevolent holler of mirthless glee while shaking his gun in the killer's face. 'You being a dim-witted blockhead don't bother me one jot. I don't need your involvement, Jake. The pastor here will write it all down for you. And if'n you refuse to sign off with your mark, I'll do it myself. After all, it only needs a cross.' Then to the non-plussed bartender, 'Go get a pencil and paper, and write down what I dictate.'

The two ex-comrades faced one another while they awaited the pastor's return. Their once amicable comradeship was now totally destroyed, replaced by a burning need for retribution on the one hand, and escape on the other. 'So what do you want me to write, mister?' the nonplussed pastor asked when he returned.

Shad slowly dictated the confession, keeping a wary eye on his quarry as Amory scribbled it down. It read:

*I, Jacob Rankin, do hereby confess to*
*the theft of a payroll bound for Fort Wisdom*
*as well as the killing of troopers and a female*
*civilian during the robbery. Lieutenant Shadrak Pickett*
*is totally innocent of deserting his post because*
*it was me that knocked him out. I now sign this*
*confession with my mark on this 4th July, 1872. X*

'Read it back to me,' Shad ordered the barman. He nodded, satisfied that it would exonerate him. Shad then carefully folded the confession and slipped it into his pocket. 'Now unfasten that gun belt and let it drop.'

Rankin's shoulders lifted in a shrug of apparent acceptance. 'Guess you've gotten the drop on me,' he balefully admitted, slowly doing as he was bidden. 'I should never have given a quick-witted guy like you the impression I was heading north. My mistake, and here I am paying for it now.' He shook his head, the cunning face simulating a look of capitulation as the unbuckled gun belt was left dangling from his right hand.

But Shad was not about to be caught out by any underhanded tactics from this snake. He backed off, giving the sly manoeuvre a mocking sneer. 'You should know better than to treat me like some rookie, Jake.' Then in a brusque tone rapped, 'Now drop the belt.'

That was the moment a young kid ran into the saloon. 'Ain't you coming out to celebrate with us, pa?' the boy called, dashing between the pair of duellists. Momentarily caught off guard by this unexpected intervention, Shad's attention was drawn to the boy. But Rankin immediately saw his chance to get the upper hand. He could have grabbed the kid and used him as a shield to escape. But that would have left Pickett able to pursue him.

Instead he pushed the boy into his foe, at the same time swinging the heavy shell belt towards Shad's face. Wrong-footed by this sudden retaliation, Shad spat out a curse while fending off the flailing belt. By saving his face from a severe gashing, he was forced to release his hold of the gun. Rankin punched out a howl of triumph as he launched himself at the impeded victim of his sly duplicity. Both men crashed into a table, which disintegrated in a heap of broken wood. But Rankin was on top and made sure he landed the first blow.

Shad tried to deflect the hard fists raining down on his unprotected body. But the unforeseen attack had put him at a marked disadvantage. A shard of wood had embedded itself in his arm, and his assailant was not about to let that benefit slip away. Being a regular soldier had turned Rankin into a capable saloon brawler, a skill that he now put to good use. Being dragged back to answer for his duplicity at a hanging tribunal was most certainly not on his itinerary.

More blows thudded into the exposed torso, and Shad's handsome profile soon resembled a slab of prime beef steak. A satisfied glint saw the brutal aggressor pulling away. There was only one way to permanently ensure he remained free: in the blink of an eye the six-shooter was drawn, the hammer dragged back, and the gun pointed at the stunned victim lying on the floor. 'You should have taken my advice, fella, and headed north for Canada,' he gloatingly declared, all set to blast off. 'Now the only place you're headed is the graveyard!' His finger tightened on the trigger.

The blast from a shotgun shattered a window inches from his head. 'You'd be well advised to leather that shooter,' a low yet even voice directed. 'There's another barrel here, and it's aimed at your head.' The threat forced Rankin to do as directed. Slowly and with careful deliberation he then turned to look at the speaker. A rattler's smile, cold and menacing, greeted his gaze. This old-timer was no mooncalf, that was for sure. Rankin kept his arms raised. Skoot Amory nodded.

'Sensible fella. Your horse is waiting patiently outside. So I suggest you eat dirt,' he hissed, jabbing the scattergun with menacing intent. Rankin was left in no doubt it would be used at the slightest provocation. 'And don't think about coming back here. Being a man of the cloth, I have divine intuition to call on should you be so minded.'

'Don't worry, your reverence, I'm going,' Rankin grudgingly conceded, grinding his teeth with frustration at the thought that his nemesis would still be dogging his trail. Hopefully the beating he had given the stubborn critter would slow him up sufficiently for Rankin to make good his escape. Outside, the noisy independence celebrations had drowned out the affray taking place in the saloon. Amory went over to the door and watched until he was satisfied the troublemaker was making good his assurance to leave Arco Butte.

'Hey, Jimmy,' he called over to his son, who was still blurry-eyed following the violent showdown. 'You okay, son?' he asked, showing concern for the boy. On receiving a stunned nod, the pair of them managed to haul up the victim of the brutal assault and get him into a chair. 'Gee whizz, pa,' the kid exclaimed, staring at the battered features leering back at him. 'We ain't never had an Independence Day like this!'

'And let's hope we don't have another one,' the pastor countered. 'You just get back to your pals now. I need to find this fella some place to rest up.'

After the boy had left, eager to regale his buddies about what he had seen, Amory dabbed the bruised features with a wet rag, wiping away most of the oozing blood. The cold water partially revived the comatose figure, who groaned as he attempted to stand up. But his wobbly legs failed to support his aching torso, and he slumped back into the chair. 'You need a sawbones, mister,' the pastor advised him. 'As a man of God I can only achieve so much. But I'm sure Doc Bonneville will recommend you rest up for a few days.'

Rheumy eyes surveyed the broken remnants of the table, and Shad's breath came in short gasps as he struggled to regain some degree of control over his pulverized frame. 'Just give me a glass of whiskey,' he muttered. 'That will set me up. Then I gotta get after that skunk.' Once again he tried to rise. This time he remained on his feet, though the pastor had to provide a welcome shoulder to lean on. Amory ardently protested, but Picket held up a hand. 'The longer I stay here,' he grunted, wincing as a spike of pain lanced through his battered frame, 'the more that killer has the chance to disappear. I have to catch him to clear my name.'

Leaning down he regained his hat and set it atop the mass of dishevelled black locks. The pastor could only shrug his shoulders in resignation. There was clearly no point in pressing his counsel any further. Pickett knocked back the glass of hard liquor in a single gulp. The warm glow suffusing his limbs certainly brought colour back into his stubble-coated cheeks.

'At least let me bind your arm and give you something to eat before you leave,' Amory suggested. 'You'll be needing a full stomach to cross the Lost John Flatts. There's nothing out there save rattlers and sagebrush. Too many travellers have headed that way and failed to reach the other side. That's how it got the name, after a guy called John Henry. An army patrol found his body just fifty yards from the only water hole serving that golddarned wilderness. It was barely recognizable after the buzzards had ate their fill.'

Pickett wasn't listening. All he could think of was catching up with the blamed skunk that did this. 'Which direction is he headed?' he asked.

'South.' The single-word reply brought a nod of satisfaction and a blood-tinged smile, which gave the appearance of a raw wound. Always south. 'And the only town in that direction is Blackfoot on the far side of the Flatts,' added the pastor. 'So you gonna eat something? My wife makes the best chilli beef stew this side of the Tetons.'

Only then did Pickett cotton to the fact that he hadn't touched a morsel of food since the day before. His stomach was rumbling like a thunderstorm, and chilli sounded good. Another half hour to recover his strength was probably good advice. 'I'm obliged, mister. Or should I call you pastor.' The mashed face once again split into a ghoulish leer. 'A gun-toting minister running a saloon. You sure ain't like no preacher I ever met before.'

'The Lord makes no distinction between those who take up the Good Book,' Amory loftily declared as he hustled away to prepare the food.

There was no answer to that wise piece of logic. So Pickett helped himself to another slug of whiskey as he waited to wolf down the grub. He then stood up and walked over to the open door of the saloon, watching the kids letting off more fire crackers. But his gaze soon focused on the trail heading south towards the notorious Lost John Flatts.

On this particular 4th July, a sight more than harmless firecrackers had been let off. Shad gently fingered the bruises on his mashed face. It felt as if he had been trampled by a herd of longhorns. He swayed clutching at the door jamb. The observant pastor saw that his injured visitor was about to keel over. He hurried across and sat him down at a table. 'You sure don't look well enough to leave here today, mister,' he said filling his glass.

Shad shrugged off the guy's evident concern for his welfare. 'I'll be all right. Just let me eat this grub and give me a few minutes. Then I'll be out of your hair.'

# SEVEN

# SNAKE BITE AND
# GOPHOR JUICE

Two days out from Arco Butte, and Shad Pickett was almost wishing he had taken up the minister's offer of a bed to rest and allow his sore body to recover from the beating. Almost – but not quite. His head still felt like a jackhammer pounding away inside his skull. And the continual jouncing of the horse did nothing to ease his aches and pains. Yet the urgent need to track down the varmint Rankin overcame any reservations he might have entertained.

But Lady Luck was still intent on giving Shad Pickett a hard time. Disaster struck when his horse disturbed a basking rattlesnake. The appaloosa reared up trying to avoid the lunging fangs. But it was too late. The deadly venom of the fully grown side-winder had already been injected into its leg. In his weakened state the rider was thrown to the ground. Sensing another dangerous predator close by the large snake writhed and hissed, its tail bones chattering out a warning as it prepared for another defence of its territory.

That was when Shad's army training kicked in. Panic was stifled, his hand palming the Remington and triggering off two shots at the swaying head and its flickering tongue. The first went wide but the second smashed the head, ripping it clean off the thick body, which continued to wriggle in its death throes. Shad's first thought was for his horse. The animal's injured leg was pawing the ground, its head drooping as the poison coursed through its body. He knew it was only a matter time before the poor creature keeled over. So he did the only considerate thing possible under the circumstances, and put the beast out of its misery with another bullet.

The grizzly episode had left him exhausted. And knowing he had now been cast afoot on the notorious Flatts did not enhance his confidence of survival in this bleak wilderness. In all directions, the flat expanse of sand stretched away to a hazy horizon, broken only by clumps of mesquite and sagebrush. And to add insult to injury, ominous black clouds could be seen scudding down from the north. A storm was imminent. The sun was blotted out. And within minutes the first heavy droplets of rain bounced off the dry desert floor.

The only course of action was to drape the water-proof bedroll tarp over his body, anchoring it to the dead horse. The makeshift shelter had only just been secured when the heavens opened. Fortune had smiled on the marooned traveller this time, in that his position was on the upper bank of the dried-out bed of the Lost John Creek. The flash storm that had blown up soon filled the creek. Continuous rain, sounding like the devil's drumbeat, hammered on the roof of the fragile refuge. All he could do was hunker down and ride it out.

The storm continued all day and into the night. Shad gave thanks to the oddball preacher for giving him some extra grub for the journey. Eventually the constant pounding on the roof of his shelter lulled him into a fitful sleep. It must have been in the early hours that he awoke. All was calm and still: the storm had thankfully abated. He peeped out into the early morning half-light that revealed a fresh world in which greenery prevailed. But that still left him cast afoot.

Crawling out of his refuge, the turbulent floodwaters in the creek prevented any chance of crossing to the far bank. Shad gave thanks to providence that had dumped him on the south side. He breathed in the fresh moist air of early morning before slinging the saddle bag over his shoulder and setting off on the journey south, ever south. Unable to carry the saddle in his current state of heath, it was sadly abandoned. Hopefully he would come across some remote settlement where a fresh horse could be bought.

In his mind, however, eating away like a hungry maggot, was the unsettling notion that in the meantime Jake Rankin was getting further away. He cursed the empty landscape for the manner in which his fate had been decreed. But there was no point in bemoaning his lot. All he could do was gird himself up for the long trek ahead. It soon became patently obvious that high-heeled riding boots were not designed for the foot slogger.

Later that morning he came across a lone Joshua tree. And pinned to it was an arrowed sign pointing south to Blackfoot. He appeared to have stumbled upon a well used trail. His feet were hurting as if the devil were stabbing away inside his boots. Exhaustion was also rapidly claiming his abused body. But at least he was heading in the right direction. He slumped down, back against the tree and immediately fell asleep.

His eyes opened. How much time had passed the avenger had no way of knowing. But some alien sound had jerked him awake. He pricked up his ears, listening intently. There it was again, the creak of leather and wood, a wagon of some sort coming along the trail from the north. He slid round the back of the tree and waited for the vehicle to appear. It turned out to be a travelling medicine show.

The purpose-built caravan with its ornately carved exterior was drawn by a pair of horses. All the accoutrements were piled up on top. Painted in a colourful rendition on the side was the name *Doctor Emile Lavelle's Travelling Medicine Show,* and underneath *featuring the lovely Belle Sunbeam.* If the alleged 'Doctor' was like many of his kind who frequented the remote frontier regions, the practitioner would dispense his own concoctions. The claim that these potions were derived from secret recipes able to cure anything from gout to whooping cough, and any other ailments suffered by his customers, was always skilfully pressed home. Shad had come across these quacks before.

The lovely Belle Sunbeam sounded as if she offered an enticing distraction aimed at persuading the gawping audience to part with their money, especially the male voyeurs. Travelling between remote towns, these shows offered other entertainments, including juggling and simple conjuring tricks, with the assistant providing a song and dance routine. All of it was geared up to selling the various cures in which each practitioner specialized. The shows were a welcome distraction from the hard, mundane life normally prevailing in frontier settlements, where proper medical attention was often in short supply.

A well dressed man of middle age sporting a grey top hat, his waxed moustache curled at the tips, was sitting upfront humming a ditty, completely unaware that he was being observed. His lazy-eyed demeanour turned to one of suspicion with the sudden appearance of a jasper who had all the makings of a ruthless bandit. Shad held up a hand to stop the wagon. 'Are you heading south?' he blurted out.

'Indeed I am, sir,' the man haughtily replied in a thick French accent. 'The name is Doctor Emile Lavelle, and I am the proprietor of this travelling medicine show. Our next destination is Blackfoot on the banks of the Snake River.'

'Well, I want a lift,' the traveller demanded. Shad was in no mood for bartering. 'I'll pay you the going rate when we get there.'

Lavelle's jaunty mood shrank to one of cynical mistrust. 'I do not think so, monsieur. I have no room for passengers. Especially those likely to cause trouble.' His gaze had quickly absorbed the newcomer's battered appearance. As a consequence his hand slid to the pocket of his jacket where a small pocket pistol rested.

Shad saw the move and immediately drew his own gun. 'I ain't asking, fella, I'm telling. Now hand over that peashooter. I'll get in the back. You drive and don't pull any fancy stunts.' The man shrugged. What option did he have but to submit?

The sly look, the shifty attitude, immediately put Shad on his guard. This was one wily coyote on whom you did not turn your back. Shad waved the gun in the guy's face to ensure compliance. 'And don't think to do the dirty on me. I got ears like a hawk. It's me that's holding all the aces now, so don't you forget it.' He then walked round to the back of the wagon, climbed up the steps and entered the gloomy interior.

Once the door closed, he was in total darkness. Striking a match to offer some light on his surroundings, he was startled to see a woman sitting up in a bunk. She was equally shocked by his sudden appearance, but made no attempt to call for help. The gatecrasher could not help noticing that she was no plain Jane, but a distinctly eye-catching picture to be sure. Locks of flowing auburn hair framed a face that would stop a rampant buffalo in its tracks.

He tipped his hat, bowing his head. 'Sorry to intrude, ma'am,' he apologized, forcing his eyes to remain open. 'My horse was bitten by a rattlesnake and I've been walking for too long. Your wagon coming along was a Godsend. All I want is a place to rest up. I won't disturb you.' Once again exhaustion was threatening to claim his battered torso. 'I'll just lie on the floor.' And without further ado, he did just that. And instantly fell asleep.

Ten minutes later, Emile Lavelle drew the wagon to a halt. He waited to see if the stranger would appear. When nothing happened, he cautiously stepped down and went round to enter the back door. 'He's not going to cause us any trouble,' the girl assured the older man. 'Look at him. He's been in a fight, judging by his condition. Help me get him up on the bunk.'

'We ought to just dump him on the trail,' Lavelle protested. 'Guys like him only bring trouble. Let somebody else help him out.'

The proprietor's heartless attitude elicited a disdainful response from the girl. 'If'n you're frightened he's gonna jump you, here...' She handed him the two guns. Lavelle had no hesitation in commandeering them. 'Satisfied?' she mocked. 'Now help me get him up. He's in need of some tender care.' A gentle hand smoothed the greasy hair off his forehead to reveal a handsome profile. Yet she couldn't help but sense that a deeply troubled persona lay beneath the battered exterior.

How much time had passed when Shad eventually opened his eyes was impossible to determine. But the sight that greeted him placed any concerns he had on the backburner. Two large brown eyes peered down at him. More interesting was the care and concern displayed by the finely honed vision of beauty. Was it all an hallucination? Surely he must still be asleep. 'I had a dream that some gorgeous apparition was cleaning me up,' he murmured holding the girl's apprehensive gaze. He shifted his weight trying to sit up. A stab of pain shot through his aching body. His eyes closed. 'Guess that's all it was after all.'

'No dream, mister,' a soft voice purred in his ear. 'Luckily there don't appear to be any serious injuries. But you're gonna be sore for a few days.'

Minutes passed before he opened his eyes again peering in the mirror she handed over. The girl was right. Although cleaned up, his face had more bruises than a rotten peach. He fingered the prominent bump on his head and winced. 'I'm obliged to you,' he said with genuine indebtedness. 'Guess you must be the gorgeous assistant, Belle Sunbeam, advertised on the side of the wagon.' He couldn't resist a wry smirk. 'Fancy handle.'

'In my line of work, having a snappy title helps sales,' she retorted. 'A girl has to earn a living some-how. I trust you have no objections?'

'Pardon me, ma'am,' Shad apologized. 'No offence intended. I kinda like it, it suits you.' Then he remembered how he had gotten here, and the reason. A ribbed frown dissolved the easy smile. 'Did I say anything while I was asleep?'

The girl relaxed, accepting the contrite regret. 'You sure were burbling some strange things. Most of it was gibberish. But needing to keep heading south seemed to crop up fairly often. It must be mighty important for you to end up like this.'

'So what was I saying?' he enquired tentatively. 'Folks can spill all kinds of drivel after they've been beaten up.'

'Oh, now let's see,' the girl considered thought-fully. 'Stuff about being wrongly hounded out the army… for cowardice. A stolen payroll. Those things ring a bell?'

Shad's face turned ashen, and assumed a distinctly worried look. How would this woman react if'n she knew all the facts? More important, would she believe him?

Belle seemed to read his thoughts. 'Don't worry none, mister,' she assured him. 'I never judge a book by its cover, even though your'n was mighty tattered before I got to work on it. Care to enlighten me on the grim details? Or is it none of my business?'

He studied her closely before replying, trying to work out how she would react to being told the truth. What he saw instilled the belief that one person at least would give him a fair shake of the dice. Added to appreciation for her compassionate manner was a yearning to take her in his arms. On this latter he held back, not wishing to give out the wrong message. Shad Pickett had always reckoned himself to be a good judge of character. And this woman appeared to exude sincerity and fidelity.

It would do him good to share the burden he had been forced to carry. 'More like a peal of bells, ma'am. Loud and clear. But it ain't what you might think. I can tell you for a fact that it certainly wasn't no illusion talking,' he snarled. An angry glint was reflected in his eyes. 'I'm tracking the fella what did this to me so I can take him back to Fort Wisdom in Montana to clear my name.' He pulled out the photograph and showed it to the girl. 'Ever come across him?'

Belle studied the depiction carefully. She frowned. 'The face seems kind of familiar, but he sure didn't look as smart as this.' Shad's eyes opened wide. He sat up ignoring the jolt in his side. 'It was while we were in Saddleback. Him and Emile were talking. I didn't pay much attention. Just a couple of guys splitting the breeze. That's all there was to it.'

Shad silently considered the revelation. The medicine show passing through Saddleback at the same time as Rankin. It could mean something. There again, maybe it was just a coincidence. A sluggish brain and aching body prevented any serious consideration of this potential clue, so he shrugged it off. Then slowly and with great deliberation he set about explaining his unwholesome recent past to the girl. Throughout the sorry tale, she listened intently without any interruption.

'And that's the honest truth, I swear,' Shad insisted, imploring the girl to accept his version of the grim events.

'That sure is a bad state of affairs,' Belle declared. Her ardent gaze had followed every facial twitch as the grim revelation unfolded. Her conclusion was that this man had indeed been the victim of a dreadful deception. 'But I believe you. All I can do is wish you well in tracking him down.' A deep sigh of relief softened the narrator's tense features. Knowing he now had one ally, and a fine-looking one to boot, gave him hope for the future. But no plans could be made in furthering their budding liaison until he had caught up with Jake Rankin and forced the critter to admit his guilt.

His bandaged head settled on the pillow, fond eyes drinking in the heavenly prospect. 'Sorry to have commandeered your bed, ma'am,' he apologized. 'Maybe I should go back on the floor…' But already his eyes had closed.

Belle tucked him in, planting a tender kiss on the rough stubbly face. 'My pleasure,' she murmured.

# EIGHT

# FATAL
# ATTRACTION

The gang of payroll robbers, led by Rube Chiptree, had made good time crossing the Lost John Flatts. The first settlement they came across was a remote homestead where Lief Karlsson and his wife Lucy worked a small piece of land growing crops and raising a few milk cows. Rube approached the wooden shack with care. He signalled the other three to wait in the cover of some cottonwoods while he carefully reconnoitred the place. The snake-eyed search told him that the place looked deserted.

He was just about to signal the others to join him when a woman emerged from the front door. Unaware of the alien presence close by, she went across to a well and pumped some water into a bucket, then went back inside the cabin. Chiptree waited a further five minutes. Nobody else appeared. So he signalled the others to join him. 'Looks like we gotten the place to ourselves,' hawked out Bucktooth Axell, tipping a half-empty bottle to his lips. 'Maybe there'll be some good pickings for us here.'

'You heard what the boss said,' Chiptree rasped, casting a snake-eyed glower towards his sidekick. 'No booze until after the payout.'

'And when's that gonna be?' the half-cut brigand snapped back. 'How do we know he ain't skedaddled with the whole caboodle for himself?'

'Jake wouldn't do that,' Kid Bassett butted in. 'You ain't been with the gang long enough to know he can be trusted to do right by us.'

'You guys are wimps,' Axell mocked. 'That guy needs telling he can't keep treating us like squaddies on a parade ground.'

'And you're gonna do it, I suppose,' Blacktail Guthrie snapped back.

'Why not?' was the caustic reply, fuelled by hard liquor. 'The arrogant sod needs bringing down a peg or two.'

'It didn't do Hook-nosed Charlie much good when he tried,' the Kid sneered. 'You gonna do any better?'

Axell scoffed at the notion. 'That screwball didn't go about it in the right way.'

Chiptree could only grit his teeth and hope this guy didn't sour their pitch. His authority was only temporary, and Axell knew it. Nevertheless he stood his ground. 'This ain't the time or place for arguing among ourselves,' he snapped out, straightening his back to assert what little clout he had been given. 'We'll go in slow and easy. All we want is to water our horses and give them some feed.' A caustic eye rested on the troublemaker in their midst. 'And there'll be no rough stuff. We don't want any trouble that will draw unwanted attention from the law.'

Axell grunted, slinging down another slug of hooch as they moved off. He could bide his time, for now. Outside the cabin, Chiptree called out the usual greeting from travellers approaching a new prospective resting place. 'Hello the house, anybody home?' he called out sitting astride his horse. 'Four weary travellers just wanting some water for their horses.'

Lucy Karlsson emerged from the cabin, her apron coated in flour. She smiled at the rough-looking quartet, not suspecting any skulduggery. She was an attractive woman of middle age who had kept herself quite trim. 'Welcome to the Rising Sun spread, strangers. There's coffee on the boil. And I've just finished baking some cinnamon biscuits. Set down and make yourselves at home.'

'Much obliged to you, ma'am,' Chiptree replied raising the brim of his hat. 'We sure are hungry jaspers. And our mounts could do with a drink as well.'

The woman pointed to a water trough. 'Come inside when you're done.' She returned Chiptree's easy-going smile. 'You fellas heading far?'

When Chiptree hesitated, it was Blacktail Guthrie who jumped in with a plausible excuse. 'We're wandering cowboys heading south for the Caribou country hoping to find work on a ranch.' That appeared to satisfy the woman who disappeared into the cabin.

Unlike the rough-hewn appearance of the outside, Lucy Karlsson had done her best to make the inner sanctum as homely as possible. Indian blankets graced the walls along with scenic pictures. 'Nice place you've got here, ma'am,' Chiptree enthused sipping his coffee.

'And these cookies are the best I ever tasted,' gushed Bassett. 'I sure am glad we stopped off here.' It was a genuine sentiment from the young outlaw.

Only the surly Axell remained unimpressed – except, that is, for the fine jewel case his beady eyes had noticed. It occupied a prominent position on the fireplace. In the devious robber's mind such a fancy possession clearly held some valuable trinkets. He stashed the discovery away while maintaining a smile that Snake-eyed Rube would have recognized to his chagrin, had he noticed.

Sometime later the gang left, expressing their thanks to the friendly homesteader who had given each of them a pack of cookies for the rest of their journey. A mile out from the Rising Sun cabin Axell declared that he had left his pack on the table. 'I won't be long, boys,' he promised the irritated Chiptree. 'You fellas just carry on and I'll catch you up.'

Back at the cabin, Lucy was clearing up when a shadow blocked the light from the doorway. She looked around, startled by this sudden appearance of the one visitor who had given her cause for concern. 'H-have you f-forgotten something?' she stuttered out, fear displayed on her delicate features.

'You could say that,' Axell sniggered moving across to the fireplace. 'Reckon I'll relieve you of this fine case.' He snatched up the container and opened it up. Greedy eyes feasted on the array of family heirlooms passed down through generations of the Swedish family. 'These will fetch a pretty good price, to be sure,' he leered.

Taken aback by this heartless response to her open-handed goodwill, Lucy Karlsson was momentarily stunned. But she was not a woman to be cowed into submission by some lowlife robber. A growl of rage bubbled up in her throat as she lunged at the odious intruder. Her fingernails raked across Axell's leering face, drawing a line of blood. Caught on the hop, the thief howled in pain, dropping the casket, the contents scattering across the dirt floor. However, this was always going to be a one-sided contest.

Axell quickly recovered, pushing his assailant away. 'You oughn't to have done that, lady,' he snarled, a grubby paw feeling the cut on his cheek. His other hand snatched the gun from its holster. 'A really bad move.' He didn't wait for a response before pulling the trigger. The woman didn't stand a chance. Two bullet holes in the chest brought her life to a brutal end.

Gathering up his ill-gotten gains, Bucktooth Axell made good his escape just as the woman's husband was returning to the ranch. Lief Karlsson knew something bad had happened after hearing the shots. Seeing a rider galloping away from the cabin with the devil on his heels only confirmed his fears. Three other riders could also be seen awaiting their buddy on a hillock on the far side of the spread. The farmer dashed into the cabin.

Total shock registered on the poor man's blanched face as he sank to his knees beside the dead woman. A choking sound that was no more than a repressed gurgle issued from a parched throat. His whole body trembled as he gently cradled Lucy in his arms. And there he stayed, rocking her, tears streaming down his face.

Eventually the true horror of his situation hit home, like the kick from a loco mule. Tight-shut eyes striving to eradicate the awful truth now opened wide. A scream of pure agony held in for too long burst forth, its heartbreaking wail shattering the grim silence and bouncing off the walls of the small room. Tough as old boots and used to dealing with misfortune, this was a calamity too far.

But Swedish pragmatism had to overcome sorrow. Now it was time for the tough, resilient homesteader to take action. His first job was the most harrowing of all. The burial of his dear Lucy in a small plot already containing their still-born child Eric was completed as if in a dream. Prayers were offered up for her dearly departed soul. Then came the part where hate and the overwhelming desire for vengeance took over.

Lief saddled a horse and took off for the nearest town of Blackfoot, which lay two hours ride to the south. Sheriff Grit Angstrum was the man to hunt these killers down. Four men on the run should not be hard to track down. And the grieving nester would enjoy nothing more than seeing them pay the ultimate price for their infamy.

\*\*\*

After Bucktooth Axell had rejoined his sidekicks, curiosity about their associate's odd behaviour was writ large across staring faces. 'So did you get them cookies you're supposed to have forgotten, Bucktooth?' Guthrie asked in a cynical tone of voice. Suspicion as to his sidekick's real motive was not concealed. Although muffled by the thick walls of the cabin, Guthrie was near certain he had heard shots.

'I'll maybe let you fellas have the answer to that question when we've quit this berg,' Axell declared, spurring his horse away after casting a wary eye to his rear. The others followed his gaze and observed a man standing outside the cabin. His agitated movements indicated that Axell's second visit had not gone down well. They didn't need any further incentive but to follow the headstrong killer over the rim of the hill. The gang wasted no time in heading into the hills back to their hideout.

A steady pace was maintained all the way over to their own less-than-salubrious hideout in Greasy Grass

Gulch. The tortuous journey lasted two full days. The gulch was a constricted rift in the landscape, the winding trail through it leading deep into the wild fastness of the Grand Tetons. So narrow was the steep-sided ravine that any progress necessitated riding in single file.

The creek was eventually swallowed up in an oval-shaped amphitheatre. At its head the hideout was well hidden, being little more than a cave at the base of a cliff face, across which a log wall complete with door and window had been built. But it offered the perfect hideout for a ruthless gang of brigands. And there they waited for the arrival of Jake Rankin.

'So what you been doing, Bucky?' Kid Bassett demanded, impatient to see why his sidekick had return to the Rising Sun. He didn't believe for one moment that it was the excuse given. Axell had maintained his secret throughout the trek to Greasy Grass, much to the impatience of his buddies.

'And don't try putting us off with some hogwash about cookies,' Chiptree interjected. A finger pointed to the twin lines of red scarring the outlaw's stubbly face. 'That woman don't appear to have welcomed your return visit.' The others smirked, murmuring their agreement while gathering round and pressing their buddy for a proper response.

With a wily smirk the killer slowly withdrew the ornate casket from his saddlebag. 'Guess you're right there, Snake,' he teased. 'She didn't take kindly to my request to relieve her of this fine prize. I ain't had a real look myself yet,' he said, slowly opening the lid and enjoying their curious looks. 'So let's take a look-see, eh boys?' Slowly he raised the lid. Inside was an array of trinkets, some of which were cheap copies. But two gold rings with what appeared to be diamonds entwined in silver filigree twinkled at the watchers.

'How in thunderation did some homesteader come by these sparklers?' Chiptree gushed, a grubby paw fingering the jewels.

'The woman claimed they were family heirlooms, but they're sure gonna net me a handsome profit,' Axell said, feasting his grasping peepers on the prizes. He fished out the bottle of hooch from his bag and tipped a hefty slug down his gullet. This time Chiptree did not object. Much as they had genuinely enjoyed the hospitality shown by Lucy Karlsson, these guys were, after all, barefaced robbers at heart.

'What about us, then?' Guthrie demanded. 'You know the rules we all agreed to. Any payoff is shared out among the whole gang.'

'You can have the pendant, Bucky,' Chiptree commented, guffawing as he turned it over, pointing to the inscription on the rear. 'Not that its gonna be much use to you: *With love from Lief to Lucy.* No chance of having your wicked way giving any dame that.'

'Unless she's called Lucy,' interjected Bassett, a remark that occasioned hearty chuckles from the others.

But the hilarity was short-lived. So engrossed had they been in examining the illicit haul that nobody had heeded the appearance of Jake Rankin. A single shot from his rifle shattered the bottle in Axell's hand. 'What did I say about no booze until the payoff?' He stalked across the yard slamming a bunched fist into the killer's face.

Axell went down, blood oozing from a cut lip. But he was not the sort to take that kind of treatment without a fight. His hand grabbed for the holstered revolver, but a rifle jabbed into his chest before he could draw. 'I ought to put a bullet in your mangy hide for this,' Rankin snarled, standing over the fallen owlhoot.

'We've waited too long already for a payout,' Axell retorted, scrambling to his feet. 'This was something extra to keep the wolf from the door.'

'You darned fool,' Rankin raged. 'You were meant to stay out of trouble. Now the whole county will be hunting us down after you killed that woman. Get on your horse and clear out. You're finished here.'

'What about my cut of the payout?' Axell railed.

Rankin stepped forwards, the long gun raised. 'Be thankful you're still breathing, lunkhead. If I see your ugly mug again you'll be eating lead. Now git!'

'You ain't heard the last of this, Rankin,' Axell blurted out, staggering across to his horse. 'Nobody does the dirty on Bucktooth Axell.'

Rankin was unfazed as he watched the killer ride off. Contempt for what he considered to be a toothless threat registered in his sneering expression. Once Axell had disappeared, he turned to address the others. 'You fellas stick around here until I get back from Blackfoot. That's where I'm due to meet Lavelle to pick up our share of the dough. There's plenty of food in the cave to keep you happy. But no drink.' He fixed a warning gaze on each man. 'That crazy coot Axell has paid the price for disobeying orders.' To further show his contempt for the leper's rash act, he tossed the casket in the dirt.

The three remaining outlaws shuffled their feet, wilting beneath the stern military bearing. But there was no respect evident in any man's gaze. Only a burning resentment at being treated like raw army recruits. Yet such was the tight control that Rankin exerted over them, none had the nerve to challenge him outright. All they could do was watch straight-faced as the gang leader mounted up and rode off.

Nobody spoke until Rankin was out of sight. It was Rube Chiptree who then expressed their mutual antipathy. 'Axell and Hooky Tapshaw were right about Rankin. The guy still thinks he's a darned drill sergeant. Soon as we get paid off I'm cutting loose. Any of you guys want to join me?'

Both Guthrie and Bassett nodded their readiness to start out afresh, free of the domineering restraints imposed by Jake Rankin. 'And I reckon we should start right now by spending that dough he so kindly gave us.' The suggestion was daubed with a thick wedge of sarcasm. 'And I for one intend to slake my fill of best scotch whiskey in the nearest saloon.'

'Yeehaah!' Guthrie yelled. 'I sure am with you there, Snake. What about you, Kid?'

Bassett concurred while picking up the casket and its contents. 'And maybe we can sell these to some poor sucker while we're down there. I'll keep hold of this bauble though,' he said twirling the pendant on his finger. 'Maybe I'll advertise for some dame called Lucy who wants to walk out with a good-looking guy like me.'

'The Kid's gonna be a greybeard afore that happens,' Guthrie sniggered to his pal, much to Chiptree's amusement. Bassett didn't take any offence, merely puffing his shoulders up in mock annoyance. It was only light-hearted joshing from his older buddies, who secretly envied the blond-haired kid's ability to snap his fingers for the girls to come a-running.

Eager to enjoy some revelry after their tough flight from Montana, no time was wasted in heading east for the nearest town, which happened to be just over the border in Jackson, Wyoming. The Blue Peacock was the first saloon encountered. With money in their pockets the three desperadoes felt as if they had been discharged from the army, such was the austere discipline Jake Rankin had instilled in his small contingent.

Admittedly he had given them no reason to complain at the spoils of their nefarious exploits over the last six months. But men like these can only take so much military-style control. And that time had run its course.

'Okay, boys,' declared Blacktail Guthrie fervently, steering his mount to the hitch rail outside the saloon. 'Let's go have us a ball!'

Whoops of delight greeted this welcome sugges-tion as they stamped into The Peacock's dim interior. A glossy painting of the bird in all its pristine glory graced the back wall of the bar. A bottle of whiskey and two glasses were ordered, half of it disappearing down Kid Bassett's gullet in minutes. 'Boy, that sure hit the mark,' Bassett enthused, smacking his lips.

'You just go easy on the hard stuff, Kid,' Chiptree advised, sipping the glass of beer he had opted for. 'We don't want you mouthing off about our business.'

The cogent advice was shrugged off. 'I ain't no greenhorn, Rube,' he burbled. 'Reckon I'll go try and get one of these dupes to buy these baubles,' he said, lumbering to his feet. Unlike his older buddies, the Kid was less able to hold his liquor, and had to hold on to the table where they were sitting.

'Easy there, Kid,' Guthrie cautioned. 'Maybe we should go find us a proper dealer.'

'Let me try the bartender,' Bassett said. 'If'n he don't bite my hand off, we'll do as you say.' He lum-bered off, dragging the items out of his pocket.

The two outlaws watched nervously as he pre-sented the goods to the barman for inspection. A serious frown crossed the rotund barkeep's face as he examined the haul. Neither of the owlhoot watchers could hear what passed between the pair at the bar. The barman called another drinker over to look at them. Following some incoherent muttering the second man pointed to the outside as if he were indicating a more likely place for a deal to be made.

Bassett nodded, collecting up the goods before returning to his edgy pals. 'That guy over yonder reckons there's a jeweller three blocks down the street who will likely buy these beauties.' The Kid sunk another slug of hooch, grinning from ear to ear. 'Drink up boys, and let's go make ourselves dough enough for some real action in this berg.'

His avid enthusiasm appeared to rub off on his two older pals. Maybe these goodies were more valuable than they had first thought. The drinks were finished. Then the three outlaws left, in the hope of sealing a profitable deal.

What they failed to heed was the barman's rapid departure from the saloon.

# NINE

# BLACKFOOT

Meanwhile the travelling medicine show was continuing to trundle south towards its next stopping-off point, which happened to be Blackfoot. Thrown together under such bizarre circumstances, the two passengers had grown close. On pressing her, the girl revealed that she had joined up with Emile Lavelle's show after his previous assistant jumped ship to marry a perfume drummer in the town of Butte.

'I had a small talent for singing and dancing in the saloons,' Belle declared, while casually lying on her bed, guilelessly revealing her most prominent assets, which Shad was hard pressed not to stare at. 'The problems arose after the show. Fending off the unwelcome attentions of pawing voyeurs got to be something I could do without.' She stretched her arms, much to Shad's discomfort. 'Emile came along at the right moment for me to quit the game. He leaves me alone. All he's bothered about is selling his patent medicines.'

'I can well understand why some guys might wish to get close,' Shad warily announced, forcing his eyes away from the said assets. 'But too many clowns exceed their authority, figuring they have the right to do as they wish. Even then they don't know the time-honoured way to inveigle themselves into a girl's affections.'

The girl sniffed imperiously. 'And I suppose you do?'

Shad lifted his hands in a calming gesture. 'Just saying, is all. The guys you've come across figure they've bought more than just your professional talents, and don't know how to behave when a lady declines their blatant propositioning. Receiving a knockback is more than they can handle. And that's when things can turn nasty.' He cut short the reasoning to study the girl's reaction.

The aloof umbrage had faded, replaced by a whimsical curiosity. 'So how would a disgraced ex-army officer go about wooing a fair maiden?' she challenged him, boldly looking him in the eye. 'Perhaps you're right. Maybe I have been associating with the wrong type of man. So let's hear your pitch, buster.'

Shad's face turned sunset orange, his brow knitting in lines thick as cattle rope. This was not the sort of situation to which he was accustomed. The acute discomfort he felt regarding his response was saved by the abrupt cessation of movement – from the steady creak and rock of a travelling wagon, stillness now prevailed. Shad hustled to the back door and peered out.

Lavelle had got down and was peering through a fence towards a homestead. Stuck on the southern edge of the Flatts where the ochre expanse of sandy wasteland had given way to more verdant pasture, this was the first settlement the passenger had come across since leaving Arco Butte three days before.

Tiptoeing up behind the stooped form of the surly showman, Shad snatched his own gun out of the guy's hand, deftly removing the pocket pistol from a shoulder holster. 'Reckon I'll take these,' he whispered casting a wary eye towards the log cabin. 'Don't want you getting any fancy notion regarding my presence, do we?' A frosty smile saw Lavelle backing off. He was joined by Belle. 'You guys stay well back until I make sure it's safe to move forwards,' he cautioned.

Shad left them both staring at the cabin as he sneaked in close to see if there was anybody about. Nothing moved. Rankin might well have passed this way. And he needed to find out if'n he was still dogging the guy's trail. He was carefully approaching the apparently empty cabin when Belle screamed out a stark warning, 'On your left by the barn!'

The homesteader was inside and had spotted what he believed to be another sneaky intruder. Maybe the same skunks who had killed his beloved wife had returned. On the western frontier, a man could never be sure of the fidelity of strangers. His wife had been far too trusting. Best to err on the safe side. Lief Karlsson raised a long gun to his shoulder. But he didn't get the chance to issue a challenge.

Belle's stark warning found Shad taking defensive action. Ducking low, he swung the Remington across his chest, triggering off a well placed shot that struck the rifle butt, forcing the man to release it. All that shooting practice on the range at Fort Wisdom had paid off. And he hadn't drawn a speck of blood, merely a sore wrist. 'What you trying to do, mister?' he demanded, advancing cautiously with the six-gun poised to deliver more of the same should the need arise. 'All I want is some information and to check if'n there is somebody home. You had no cause to gun me down.'

'I had every right,' the homesteader retorted angrily while rubbing his hand. 'You could be one of those blamed outlaws returning to rub me out.'

Shad's back stiffened. This had to be the work of the Rankin gang, passing through to meet up with the chief snake himself. 'I ain't one of them,' he hurriedly assured the nester. 'The opposite, in fact. I'm after taking them back to face justice for a past crime.'

'You a lawman?' the man asked suspiciously. 'I don't see no badge.'

'That's 'cos I'm working under cover,' Shad quickly dreamed up the fabrication. 'How many were there? Did you see their faces?' He was eager to learn as much as possible to aid his quest, which appeared to be getting closer to a showdown.

But the nester was no help on that score. 'I came back too late.' His shoulders slumped in dejection as he pointed over to a small plot where a forlorn bunch of flowers adorned a grave surmounted by a homemade cross. 'And after Lucy had made them welcome, their thanks were to kill her and steal the family jewel casket. It makes my blood boil. Only a few days after we held a party to celebrate Independence, and this happens.'

The tough farmer couldn't hold back the tears. Shad could only stand by and silently sympathize. He waited a moment before quietly asking, 'How did you know it happened?'

'I saw three riders waiting on yonder ridge. Didn't pay no mind at first. That was before I saw one of them scuttling away from the cabin like a rat up a drainpipe to join his pals. I knew something was wrong then. Cowardly killers, that's all they are. I went into the house and saw the pots left on the table…'

Karlsson paused, swallowing, as the ghastly memory flooded back. 'And there was poor Lucy lying on the floor. That skunk must have come back after seeing the jewel case and figuring there were easy pickings to be had. They weren't worth much to anyone else, but were like the English Crown Jewels to us.'

The two men walked across to the grave. The name of Lucy Karlsson had been burned into the wood. 'Your wife was a mite naïve, if'n you don't mind me saying, Mister Karlsson,' Shad remarked, trying to keep the rebuke out of his voice.

The homesteader didn't notice, responding with a dejected nod. But a burning glint of hate was evident in the man's tightly clenched fists. 'I reported it to the sheriff in Blackfoot. Grit Angstrum ain't called that for nothing. Him and the posse will catch up with them murdering skunks, come what may. And when they do, I'll be holding the rope that jerks 'em to hell. That is, if'n they don't put up a fight, then I'll be pissing on their graves.'

'I'm truly sorry for your loss,' Shad sincerely declared, handing the rifle back to its owner. He laid a comforting hand on the man's shoulder. There was nothing more to be said, so they parted without another word. Lief Karlsson remained staring at the grave, lost in a world where nought but a lonely future was all he had to contemplate. The victim was still there when the medicine wagon trundled past. No indication was given that he was aware of its passing, such was the depth of his grief.

Shad Pickett's narrowed gaze told the concerned girl that he was more than ever determined to pursue his vendetta to its conclusion. But one major obstacle had now been thrown in Shad's way: would the posse led by the doggedly determined Grit Angstrum stymie his chance for personal justice? There was no way of determining that unwholesome possibility until he reached Blackfoot and reconnoitred the lie of the land.

He posed the notion raised by the unsavoury meeting with Lief Karlsson: 'How far are we from

Blackfoot?' Before Belle could reply an excited shout from up front by Lavelle provided the answer. 'Get yourself ready, Belle. We're only five miles from Blackfoot. We should be there in two hours.' Peering out of the door, they perceived an arrowed sign nailed to a tree.

'Here's where I start earning my crust,' the girl said. 'You go sit on the back stoop while I'm changing.' She wagged a gently reproachful finger at him. 'And no peaking.'

'Tough job,' he countered with a wry smile. 'But I'll do my best.'

\*\*\*

The undulating, hilly nature of the approach to Snake Valley meant that it was three hours before they had crested the last rise. And there below on the banks of the river at its narrowest point lay the town of Blackfoot, where a bridge spanned the serpentine watercourse. From their elevated position the town appeared to be quite substantial. 'We should make a good profit here, Belle,' Lavelle enthused, seeing dollar bills floating before his avaricious eyes. 'You make sure to get the punters around when we set up shop, girl.'

'Don't I always,' the girl sighed, giving Shad a weary look. 'He gets a mite tetchy when we enter a new town,' she whispered to the passenger, who struggled to avert his own ogling peepers from the girl's scant outfit. Her effect on him went totally unheeded. 'It's only the nerves talking. He don't mean no harm.'

Shad shrugged off any desire he had to stick around. Any potential entanglement of a romantic nature could not be entertained – certainly not until he had cleared his name. Although shaking off the mesmeric effect this woman had induced in him would not be so easy to discard.

The wagon rattled its merry way down the slope and across the river's floodplain before jouncing across the wooden bridge to enter the main street of Blackfoot. As soon as they were inside the town limits, Shad said his goodbyes to the girl. Belle sadly realized this could be their last meeting when he bid her a swift 'adios' and jumped off the back of the wagon. 'You take care of yourself, mister,' she heard herself muttering as he disappeared into the curious crowd that was now walking alongside this unusual spectacle. It wasn't often that such entertainment came to town.

Lavelle cranked up the barrel organ to announce their arrival. The melodious rendition of a popular tune was rather tinny, but certainly succeeded in gaining the attention of those within earshot. 'It's showtime, Belle. We've got work to do,' he called out. 'Get your pretty ass out here and gather in the punters.' No sign of any regret was expressed that they had seen the last of their unexpected passenger.

After emerging from the rear door, Shad dropped off the wagon and quickly lost himself in the gathering crowd. Lavelle pushed on, waving a union flag until he spotted a piece of open ground ideal for setting up the show. A flat board was quickly pulled out, supported by hinged beams, providing a makeshift stage. All the while Belle was sashaying around displaying her own unique talents for the benefit of the ogling male spectators. After switching off the music, Lavelle got down to business.

'Ladies and gentlemen,' he began, holding up his hands to hush the babble. 'I, Doctor Emile Lavelle, am exceedingly privileged to stand before you today for the purpose of curing any ills from which you may be suffering.' He held up a half-empty bottle of black liquid. 'I myself am a regular imbiber of this unique restorative handed down through generations of family medical experts.'

He paused to take another drink of tantalizing elixir as the enthralled crowd goggled. 'Coughs, sneezes… even flatulence. All can be cured using my potions.' He paused to allow the laughter to die down. 'You would never guess that I stand here before you, a man of eighty-six, but looking forty years younger. You too can reduce the years by partaking of this magical potion.'

A finger then pointed to an older gent in the crowd. 'And for you, sir, an end to that awful constipation from which I know you have been suffering.' He lifted up another bottle of blue liquid. The man in question reddened, but could not deny the suggestion. This trick had never yet failed Lavelle. 'And to apologize for any embarrassment I may have caused, here…' He handed over the bottle. 'A free sample, with my compliments. And be assured it will most certainly relieve your discomfort.' The man in question gratefully accepted the bottle before disappearing into the crowd. Others immediately hurried forwards to buy the curative.

All the while Belle was circulating across the stage flaunting her generous proportions while flourishing a tub of ointment. 'And see here, my assistant Miss Belle Sunbeam…' His blue top hat was removed with a flourish as he gave the lady in question a gallant bow before continuing the eloquent eulogy. 'A woman in all her youthful glory – yet who could have supposed that in reality she is sixty years of age, her young looks thanks to Lavelle's patent beauty treatment.' This certainly caused a sensation among the female onlookers. A genuine-looking birth certificate was removed from his coat, and waved in front of the gaping throng.

Oohs and aahs went up from the older women, who eagerly pushed forwards holding out their five-dollar bills. Not to be outdone by their wives, ageing greybeards eager to regain lost vigour were no less enthusiastic. Lavelle quickly accepted the money as the concoctions rapidly disappeared.

'Fear not, folks,' he then intoned. 'I have another case of this fine tonic in the wagon.' Belle quickly left the stage, returning with the alleged final case. 'And for those of you suffering from strains, itches, twitches, gout and arthritis, the cripples and decrepit among you, we have potions to cure any complaint.'

He then held up a hand, a serious look gracing the alleged octogenarian features. 'These cures are guaranteed, but they do not happen overnight. You can, however, expect first class results to start changing your life within a week. Thereafter you will be dancing a jig of gratitude that Doctor Emile Lavelle's Medicine Show has passed through your delightful town.' Numerous reaching arms couldn't wait to hand over the fee that was going to change their lives.

But then a certain familiar face appeared in the crowd, and Lavelle's eyes widened. 'You take over, Belle. I got some business that needs sorting. Soon as this lot have been satisfied, pack everything up. Then we'll go park the wagon.' Before she could reply, he slipped off the stage, gesturing for the newcomer to join him over to one side. Belle frowned as she, too, recognized the man. What could Emile have been doing with this jasper? The meeting was no chance encounter between two buddies. Something was afoot of which she had no inkling.

On that same street, Shad Pickett was ambling along away from the medicine show, listening to numerous fiery conversations. All of them were about the recent incident at the Karlsson place. 'Those darned killers need stringing up when the posse catches them,' was a common theme. 'We don't need no trial to show the skunks how we deal with their kind of scum in

Idaho.' These people sure were heated up. And he couldn't blame them.

If'n the posse managed to run these varmints to ground and bring them back, the sheriff was going to have big trouble on his hands. The old law of the vigilante was rearing its ugly head in Blackfoot. Bar-room courts where guilty and innocent alike had little chance of a fair hearing when bloodlust was rampant were still alive and thriving in many out-back settlements, and this appeared to be the case in Blackfoot. Even had Shad been sympathetic to that kind of justice, having his quarry become the victim of a kangaroo tribunal was not part of his plan. He needed the guy alive.

# TEN

# REVENGE IS SWEET...

Mulling over the implications of the ugly mood growing ever more vociferous in the town, Shad's thoughts were jerked back to the present when the angry threats of instant justice were cut short. All eyes were turned towards the east end of town. 'It's the posse,' a voice called out. 'They've caught the killers.' As one, the crowd surged down the street like an unstoppable tidal wave. Shad joined them. The six-man posse led by Sheriff Grit Angstrum were leading three horses, each with a body tied across the saddle.

Shad sucked in a deep lungful of air. There would be no hanging today. But was one of them Jake Rankin? That was the unsettling question bubbling inside his head. He pushed forwards, eager to learn the grim truth. The crowd were keen to learn the facts behind the confrontation and the gun battle that had followed. While the lawman arranged for the bodies to be taken down to the mortuary, eager watchers surrounded the posse, hauling them into a nearby saloon. Free drinks were plied on the heroes of the moment as the facts emerged.

All Shad was bothered about was if one of them was his quarry. Then a sigh of relief issued from between gritted teeth. He had never set eyes on any of these men before. So Jake Rankin was still at large. A good thing to be sure, but that still meant he needed tracking down. And judging by the comments he had heard, no mention was made regarding the recovery of the stolen payroll. Once again Rankin had beaten everybody to the punch.

Shad was back to square one. Having eluded the posse, the guy could be anywhere by now. And surely he must have taken the loot with him. Shad's shoulders slumped and his jaw dropped as he headed for a different saloon. But then he changed his mind.

Curiosity regarding how the gritty sheriff had managed to track down and confront the gang could not be ignored. Along with numerous inquisitive citizens he entered The Longhorn saloon and stood at the back, listening intently as the facts were unfolded by a posse man who was more than ready to reveal all while clutching a glass of five-star brandy.

It turned out that the trinkets offered to the dealer in Jackson by the gang were initially accepted at face value and a price agreed. But then the man noticed

113

the engraving on the back of the pendant. He had known the Karlsson family for years and immediately guessed the truth. These men had stolen the items: Lucy Karlsson would never have surrendered these treasured possessions voluntarily. The man somehow maintained a straight face. He delayed the sale by claiming the need to obtain sufficient funds from the bank in Alpine. This would take a couple of days to arrive. So the men would have to stick around a while longer. Instead he reported directly to the mayor, who also happened to own The Longhorn saloon. A rider was despatched to get the nearest law man based in Blackfoot. On the way he chanced upon Grit Angstrum and his men, which saved time. The gun battle that ensued was a one-sided affair, and no quarter was given.

Once he had obtained the bare essentials of the showdown, Shad had no desire to hang around listening to the details of the gunfight, amply embellished for the benefit of a rapt audience. The Wayfarer saloon further down the street offered the ideal retreat for a much needed drink. The saloon was empty, save for one drinker playing patience at a table.

He shuffled over to the bar and ordered a whiskey. A Chinese bartender served him, a frown creasing the yellow features. The newcomer failed to notice the probing stare with which he was being scrutinized. All his mindful attention was centred on the whereabouts of Jake Rankin. The guy could still be close by. All of Shad's intuition now pointed to Blackfoot being the key to resolving his chilling mission. This was where they were all headed.

It came as a startling wrench to the system when the bartender bent his ear: 'Shad Pickett,' he said in the sing-song dialect of his race, tempered by an American drawl. Instantly on his guard, Shad stiffened, a hand reaching for his gun. 'Easy there, old friend,' the barman said, lowering his voice to a whisper. 'Don't you recognize me?'

Shad's brow furrowed as he looked more closely at the pig-tailed bartender. Then a light shone in his eyes. 'Foo Chang, what in blue blazes are you doing way out here in the wilds? Last time we met up was down south at Fort Animus, Durango!'

'I came north after you boys quit the fort to tackle the Indian problem on the Bozeman Trail. Been up here five years now. It's a nice town. But this business with the Karlsson household has stirred up a right hornets' nest. Folks are burning with indignation.'

'I can well understand that,' Shad added, concurring with his old associate. 'Lief Karlsson was mighty cut up about it when I passed through earlier today.'

'They were very popular around here,' Chang replied. 'A barn dance was held every month at their place, which most everybody attended. It was me that supplied the liquid refreshments.' Chang shook his head, the pigtail swaying like a flag in the wind. 'The murder of poor Lucy has hit folks badly.'

'The posse just brought in the killers over their horses,' Shad explained. 'But they've missed the one skunk I'm hunting down.'

'I heard about that business you had at Fort Wisdom,' Chang observed in a hushed voice. 'It's in the local paper. I know what they've printed ain't the Shad Pickett I knew. You being labelled a coward is just a blamed lie. But you're best not letting anybody here find out who you are, due to the present mood in town. If'n Angstrum had brought those fellas in alive, there could have been big trouble.'

'How about the whiskey, chink!' The surly demand came from the saloon's other patron. Chang quickly moved off to serve the man.

Shad slung back his own drink, nodded to the Chinaman and left the saloon. Had the drinker raised his eyes, Bucktooth Axell would have had the shock of his life. But his gaze was focused on the bottle clutched in his hand. Shad, on the other hand, could not have identified him as one of the killers because he had no idea who they were. Only Jake Rankin was known to him.

And as the homesteader, Lief Karlsson, had spotted four men fleeing the scene of their crime, he had assumed that number was the gang's composition, the obvious conjecture being that only Rankin had escaped. He was completely ignorant of Axell's ejection from the Greasy Grass hideout. Yet here Axell was, nursing a simmering hatred for the man who had done the dirty on him. Axell had known all along that sooner or later the skunk Rankin would come to Blackfoot. The drink-soused outlaw snarled, an ugly grimace scarring his warped features. And when he did, Bucktooth Axell would be ready. The venomous need for settling the score was burning a hole in his black heart.

Axell's bleary eyes eventually lifted from the now empty bottle. And that was when he received a heart-stopping shock: there, sidling along on the far side of Fremont Street, was none other than his nemesis – the treacherous, double-crossing Jake Rankin. He shook off the dulling effects of the drink and lurched to his feet. Here was his big chance to get revenge on the bastard. Shad had left The Wayfarer moments before, and so failed to notice him.

Axell slid out of the saloon. A circuitous course through numerous back lots ensured that he would reach his destination, the sheriff's office, without being spotted. Hiding in an adjoining alley, the vengeful predator waited until his foe could be seen ambling down the street. For some reason Rankin was heading for the north end of Blackfoot. Like his old sidekicks, Axell was ignorant as to where the payroll was now.

All that mattered at that moment was getting his revenge on the bastard. And here was his chance. The outcast attempted a smile more akin to a malicious leer, one that displayed his jutting gnashers like two snapping fangs.

He emerged from hiding, carefully edging along the boardwalk. All the while he maintained a watchful eye on Rankin, whose attention was focused on reaching his own destination. 'This is where you get what's coming to you, scumball,' the ousted owl-hooter growled under his breath. 'Nobody pisses in my face and gets to walk away.'

He then slid into the law office. Two minutes later he emerged accompanied by Sheriff Angstrum and his deputy Flick Gallatin. 'There's the killer who escaped your posse, sheriff,' Axell gleefully extolled pointing a damning finger at the back of Jake Rankin. 'He's the one who fired the shot that killed that homesteader's wife.'

'Are you certain about this?' Grit Angstrum cautioned. He did not want to arrest an innocent man.

'I saw it all from a hill overlooking the cabin,' Axell insisted. 'I ain't no gunfighter, just a drifting cowpoke looking for work so I didn't want to challenge him. But it was him all right. No mistake. I got eyes like a hawk.' That was enough for the tenacious lawman who stepped down ready to tackle the killer head on.

The openly hostile declaration had attracted a host of spectators. Immediately the cry went up. 'The last of them blamed killers has been caught!' Within seconds a large crowd had surrounded the figure of the stunned Jake Rankin. 'Hang the murdering rat!' The frenzied cry was taken up by a myriad throats, and as if by magic a rope was produced and slung around the victim's neck.

Angstrum and his deputy were overwhelmed. Only half way across the street and they were pushed aside by the ugly mood of the crowd. An unstoppable demand for instant mob justice had been initiated and was now in full flow. Only a miracle could prevent hate-induced mayhem from swallowing up any rational judgement.

The gritty tin star, however, was not prepared to let vigilante law rear its ugly head in his town. He went to draw his revolver. But there was no gun in his holster, nor that of his deputy. Both had been surreptitiously snatched by those eager for their own brand of retribution. Rabble-rousers had taken charge. 'Take him down to the hanging tree.' The rabid howl was taken up by the hostile crowd. Mob rule was rampant, and nothing was going to stand in its way.

Rankin was roughly dragged along. His shouts claiming his innocence were drowned out by the mob's ghoulish desire for blood. On one side, removed from all the mayhem, Axell was relishing his old boss's fate. And with his three pals lying on a cold slab in the mortuary, all that stood between him and a fortune in greenbacks was that old has-been Emile Lavelle. He spat in the dust. Nothing was going to stop him seizing the entire caboodle for himself. But first he would enjoy watching Rankin kick out his life on the end of a rope.

The uproar down the street attracted Shad Pickett's attention just before he entered The National Hotel. He paused with a hand resting on the door handle. The need for rest and recuperation was eclipsed by the menacing clamour that had suddenly blown up further back along Fremont Street. The muttered imprecations that had initially heralded the arrival of the three dead outlaws was nothing compared to this. Something bad must have occurred to cause such a disturbance. He hurried back along the boardwalk in time to see the mob coming towards him. The hostile procession was clearly headed for a prominent tree occupying its own plot of land between a hardware store and saddlery.

Far more startling to Shad Pickett, and eminently alarming, was the presence of Jake Rankin with the noose of a hanging rope slung round his neck. So Blackfoot had been his destination after all. And some bizarre fluke had found him charged with Lucy Karlsson's murder. How in tarnation had that come about? Shad's brow furrowed as he checked the date on the written confession. There was no mistake: it was the 4th July.

So Rankin had been in Arco Butte on Independence Day. And it was a four-day ride from the homestead. Guilty as sin of the Pioneer Road massacre, he was about to be lynched for another crime he had not committed. What in blue blazes had happened to make this frenzied mob think Rankin was the killer?

The answer was close by on the opposite side of the street, in the person of the hard-boiled jasper with the ear-slitting grin plastered across his leering face: standing alone and removed from the angry tumult, Bucktooth Axell could not contain his elation.

The damaged reputation of the cashiered officer had in no way affected his logical thinking process, and Shad instantly reasoned that this fella had to be the real killer, the one whom Lief Karlsson had witnessed riding away from the homestead. Rankin must have found out and kicked him out of the gang before heading for his rendezvous in Blackfoot. Now the vengeful villain was getting his own back. And with all the other members of the gang dead and gone, he would be expecting a big payout all for himself.

And in minutes the skunk would have his wish granted, and Shad Pickett would be left rudderless on a storm-tossed sea, his one chance of redemption snuffed out by another miscarriage of justice. The irony of the bleak situation was hard to comprehend. The prospect of a life, if'n it could be so called, living in the shadow of wrongful disgrace, and being cold-shouldered by his fellow men, stretched away into a dismal future. Shad Pickett could not allow that to happen. Something must be done, and quickly.

# ELEVEN

# ...BUT ONLY IF
# SUCCESSFUL!

Unarmed and therefore helpless to stop the ill-omened threat of anarchy from invading his town, Grit Angstrum and his deputy had hurried back to the law office to rearm themselves. But they would be too late to prevent an 'innocent' man being hanged for the wrong crime: his sentence should have been left for a military tribunal to carry out. Unless Shad Pickett could do something to intercede, disaster would surely prevail. But what to do? He looked around, anxiously willing some means of intercession to present itself.

And there it was, standing outside a feed store: a stationary wagon with four horses waiting patiently in the traces. The driver must have abandoned his task to join the crowd. Without further thought, Shad ran across and leapt up on to the front seat. Grabbing hold of the reins, he slapped the team into motion and swung the wagon round in a tight circle so that it faced the oncoming mob. Heading straight for the crowd, he urged the team into a gallop. Only at the last minute did the leading vigilantes spot the danger rampaging towards them. Panic gripped them, and the instinct for survival took command.

Men were scattered in all directions like wind-blown chaff as the wagon thundered past. With his hands tied behind his back and hindered by the odious necktie, Rankin was left floundering on the ground. The wagon ploughed on, not stopping until it had rounded a corner and was out of sight. Only then did Shad abandon his position. He hurried back to the corner and peered up Fremont Street to discover if his ploy had succeeded.

A sigh of relief issued from betwixt his pursed lips. The sheriff and his deputy, accompanied by a couple of the more peaceable citizens, had taken control. With mob rule broken up, the sheriff marched the prisoner over to the jail. Some of the more verbose rebels followed, hurling threats of further action at Angstrum's back. But their nerve had been shattered by the mysterious intervention of the runaway wagon.

'All we want is justice, sheriff,' Walt Freeman, the local butcher, demanded. 'We can't allow that skunk to hire some smart-ass lawyer to get him off the hook.'

Once on the boardwalk outside his office, the sheriff swung round to face the petulant big-mouths.

'There'll be no vigilante law in this town,' the burly starpacker declared with vigour. The stark warning was backed by the twin-barrelled scattergun pointing at the speaker. 'You'll have justice, Walt, never fear on that score. But it will be carried out by a proper court hearing.'

'You fellas have got this all wrong,' Rankin butted in, pleading his innocence. 'I never killed that woman. You've gotten the wrong man.'

'Tell that to the judge, mister,' Deputy Gallatin snapped. 'He'll be here to conduct the case in two weeks.' And with that the accused culprit was hustled inside the jailhouse. 'And don't be figuring he'll let you off the hook, 'cos we have a witness who saw you do it.'

That was when Rankin saw the light. 'Axell,' he muttered under his breath. Then in a loud angry voice, he yelled out a virulent threat. 'Axell, you treacherous rat. Think you can shop me and get away scot free? I'll stuff those buckteeth down your lying throat, then drag you to burn in Hell with me. You hear me, scumbag?' This final admonition was torn from Rankin's throat as he was dragged inside the jailhouse by Flick Gallatin.

'The show's over, folks,' the sheriff declared, firmly holding his shotgun in full view to emphasize the shift of authority back into his hands. 'Get about your business and let the law take its rightful course.' With much muttering, the crowd dispersed. Angstrum sighed with relief. That sure was a close call. Only then did he wonder about the mystery wagon that had fortuitously prevented the breakdown of law and order.

Curiosity found him wandering down the street and round the far corner. And there was the wagon with a local farmer scratching his head. 'This your wagon, Zeke?' the sheriff asked. He didn't wait for an answer. 'Was it you who drove it through that crowd planning to take the law into their own hands back yonder?'

The farmer shook his head still clawing at his scalp. 'Don't know how it got down here, sheriff,' he exclaimed, total bewilderment creasing his weathered face. 'This is where I found it a few minutes ago.'

There was nobody else in the vicinity. Now it was the turn of Grit Angstrum to scratch his head. A mystery, to be sure. If he ever did find out who the driver was, the town's gratitude would be expressed. But until then it would have to remain an unsolved conundrum.

Standing on the edge of the small crowd that was now dispersing, Shad was also cognizant of the name Axell. Bucktooth Axell had been one of the jaspers that his old sergeant had been illegally involved with at Fort Wisdom. With the other three in the mortuary, that meant there had to be five outlaws who had attacked the payroll detail. Rankin was now safely locked up, so that left Axell the only one still free to get his hands on the loot. But not if Shad Pickett had any say in the matter. Those bunny-like choppers were the ones he had seen across the street only minutes before. He hurried back in time to see Axell disappear into The Wayfarer. He clearly intended celebrating his treachery before claiming the prize. Here was Shad's chance to tackle the bastard.

But he needed an edge to catch the skunk off guard. Slipping down the adjoining alleyway behind the saloon, he located a door. It was unlocked and gave access to a store room full of empty beer barrels. Slowly and with careful deliberation he sidled over to the door opposite that gave access to the bar. It was slightly ajar so he pushed it, praying that the hinges did not squeak. Luck was with him.

He stepped through, sneaking a watchful peak towards his prey. Apart from Axell the saloon was still empty. No sign of Chang. The barman's absence had encouraged the skunk to help himself. His back was to Shad as he reached up and commandeered two bottles of best Scotch whiskey. No money was placed on the counter.

Shad's mouth tightened in disgust as he stepped into view. 'Once a thief, always a thief, as well as a dirty killer, eh Bucktooth?' he snarled, standing square on, the gun steady in his hand. Axell swung round on his heel, mouth agape. His eyes widened as he stared like a landed fish at this spectre he had figured was past and gone. 'I see you recognize me,' observed Shad, his deadpan look harbouring all the revulsion amassed as a result of that horrendous incident. 'It should have been you out there about to hang on that tree, not Jake. But I have other plans for him. Now lift that gun out nice and slow, then toss it away.'

That was when Axell found his voice. 'You got this all wrong, mister,' he blustered, attempting to deny any wrongdoing. 'The barman has gone out so I served myself. But I was going to pay for these.' It was a weak excuse while the killer figured out how to extricate himself from this unexpected obstacle to his plans.

'Chuck the hogleg or I'll plug you here and now,' Shad rasped, jabbing his own shooter. Axell was given little choice but to obey. The gun clattered as it skidded across the wooden floor. Shad replaced his own gun. He wanted to take this critter alive.

But the killer was not beaten yet. No way was he going to surrender now, when all that dough was just waiting to burn a hole in his pockets. The tension in the empty room crackled, both men sensing that a climax to this stand-off was imminent.

Still holding one of the whiskey bottles, Axell aimed it at Shad's head. The sly move had been expected – no way was the avenger going to be taken by surprise a second time. A quick shift to the left saw the bottle flying past his head and shattering against the wall. He then unbuckled his own gunbelt and laid it aside. 'I want you alive, peabrain,' he growled out flexing his fists. 'You're gonna stand trial for Lucy Karlsson's murder, and not Rankin. I'm taking him back to Fort Wisdom to clear my name. But first you're gonna tell me where that dough is hidden.' Shad then launched himself at the killer. But Axell was no easy antagonist.

He backed off, drawing a knife from a boot sheath. An ugly grin delivered the ultimatum that no mercy would be shown. Jabbing at his opponent, he forced Shad on to the defensive, while the deadly blade swished perilously close to Shad's face. But the momentum caused Axell to stumble, allowing Shad to grab his knife hand. Both men wrestled, each desperately trying to gain an advantage.

Shad managed to slam the killer's hand against the wall, but he refused to release the knife. His free hand came round, punching Shad in the face. A sharp pain lanced through his cheek. A second punch blurred Shad's vision. Too late he concluded he should have shot the critter out of hand. What had he been thinking? Trying to play by the rules and be a law-abiding citizen, right-minded with principles, had gotten him nowhere, either with the tribunal or these killers. Better to play dirty, just like them.

Now it was a plain matter of survival that found him desperately hanging on. Somehow in the tussle he managed to slam an elbow in the killer's face, enabling him to push his assailant away. That gave Shad the time to dodge behind a table, earning him a brief chance to think. His leg shot out, striking the edge of a chair that cracked against the knife-wielder's legs. Axell cried out and staggered back, the weapon slipping from his fingers.

The balance of power had shifted once again, and Shad took full advantage. Throwing the table aside he stepped forwards, letting fly a concrete punch that rocked the killer back on his heels. A second jab followed up, flooring the critter.

With the advantage now in Shad's favour, he had no intention of relinquishing it. But Axell wasn't finished yet. His right hand somehow found the abandoned pistol, and he grasped the butt. It rose, along with the killer. Somewhat unsteady on his feet, the bucktoothed leer caused a chilling ripple to run down his opponent's spine. The hammer snapped back to full cock, and his finger tightened on the trigger.

All seemed lost when a small figure darted out of an open door at the other end of the bar and smashed a club over Axell's head. His eyes bulged and rolled up into his head as he crumpled and fell to the floor. Foo Chang stood over the braggart, holding the club aloft, his slitted eyes gleaming, ready to deliver another blow should it be needed. But Axell was out for the count.

For Shad Pickett, history was repeating itself. He breathed deep, allowing his heart rate to settle. This was the second time his life had been saved while on the brink of being snuffed out, first by Pastor Kloot Amory, and now Foo Chang. And then there was the lovely Belle Sunbeam who had nursed him back to health. He felt like the cat with nine lives. Surely such good fortune could not last. Next time might well prove that three lives were all he had been granted.

For now, all he could do was thank his guardian angel in the guise of the little Chinaman. 'I owe you my life, buddy,' he gasped out, gripping the little guy's shoulder. Chang grinned, basking in this praise, such as rarely came his way, and accepting the wicked-looking bowie. It looked like a meat cleaver in his tiny hands, but caused Chang great delight as he waved it in the face of the comatose loser of the fracas.

Looking around Shad spotted the bucket of water that all saloons kept handy to tackle the ever-present danger of fire. He tossed the greasy contents over the sprawled figure on the floor, and the liberal dousing had the desired effect of bringing Axell to his senses. He groaned aloud, unsure of his whereabouts. Only when he was fully conscious did Shad go to work on him: he was soon securely tethered to a chair.

'You're gonna tell me where that payroll is, dog breath,' Shad rasped, standing over him. 'Otherwise I'll set Foo here on you.' The Chinaman danced around grinning inanely, waving the large knife in his face. 'Guess I don't need to remind you how imagina-tive these guys can be when it comes to inflicting pain.' A stream of giggles bubbled from Chang's animated face as he tested the razor edge of the deadly blade. Axell's face blanched in terror. The application of cold steel is apt to focus a villain's mind. 'So are you gonna talk, or do I leave you in Chang's capable hands?'

To ensure he complied, Chang nicked Axell's nose, drawing blood, which dribbled down into his mouth. That was enough for Bucktooth Axell to blurt out the truth. He explained that after the robbery, the gang had headed for Saddleback to meet up with Emile Lavelle, where the payroll was transferred to his wagon until it could be shared out. And that was to be here, in Blackfoot. When pressed, Axell nervously insisted, under threat of a carve-up, that since Rankin booted him out of the gang, he had no idea where the medicine wagon was now. The fact that it had already reached Blackfoot was clearly unknown to him.

The muscles of Shad's face tightened as the grim truth unfolded. So the medicine wagon and Rankin's gang arriving in Saddleback at the same time was no chance encounter. It was a planned meeting to hide the stolen payroll. His whole body trembled. Who would ever suspect a travelling medicine show of carrying the loot until it could be shared out among the bandits? And that snake of a showman Lavelle was hand-in-glove with them.

Shad was dumbfounded. And all the time he was in the wagon recovering from that beating, the payroll was within touching distance. That said, an unwholesome doubt clouded his euphoria at learning the truth. Was Belle Sunbeam in cahoots with the gang? Had all that kindness been just a ruse to get rid of him at the earliest opportunity? He could barely credit that she could be one of the outlaws. The woman had seemed so genuine. But his first priority now was to find out where the payroll had been stashed. It had to be somewhere in Blackfoot. And by now Lavelle must be aware of Rankin's arrest.

'I'm off to locate where that medicine wagon has been stashed,' he said to Chang, handing over Axell's revolver. 'Best you have his gun as well, old friend,' Shad advised. 'Keep this critter under close watch until I get back. Have you gotten some place to hold him?' The little guy nodded: 'My cellar is better than any jail.'

Axell's pleading eyes beseeched his captor not to leave him alone with this manic torturer. Shad couldn't resist a morbid grin, purposely ignoring the appeal while enjoying the rat's discomfort. He then left the saloon and headed slowly along the street, wondering where to begin his search.

With all his attention concentrated on the arrest of Jake Rankin and now Bucktooth Axell, Shad was unaware that Belle Sunbeam had joined him. A light hand rested on his shoulder – but her unexpected touch triggered an instinctive reaction to danger, and he swung round, grabbing her arm and jamming his gun into her midriff. Her cry of alarm elicited a babbling apology when he realized his error.

'Jeepers, ma'am, I sure am sorry for acting like that.' The gun was quickly holstered, contrition drawing a heartening smile of acceptance from this dazzling ray of light. 'You gave me quite a start, coming up like that. I'm a mite jumpy at the moment.' He didn't elaborate on his capture of Axell. There was the thorny problem of finding Emile Lavelle and the stolen money.

But his joy at seeing her was tempered by a suspicion regarding her possible involvement with the thieves. However, she didn't appear to notice the sudden chill in the air, and declared: 'I didn't mention it before when you showed me Rankin's picture because I forgot that while we were in Saddleback, four other men were hanging about waiting.' Shad was all ears, his eyes gleaming with expectation as she continued: 'One of them had bunny teeth, which stuck in my mind.'

Shad stifled a sigh of relief. This further elaboration appeared to prove her innocence regarding any association with the gang. Axell's admission regarding the participation of Lavelle was now relayed to her by Shad, who vigilantly studied the girl's reaction. Even a good actor could not have faked her shock when she learned her partner was a crook in league with a bunch of killers. The blood drained from her cheeks, leaving a blanched stare. Shad was now fully convinced that she was an innocent dupe in the perpetration of the heinous crime.

Her disbelief that she could have been so gullible and so callously hoodwinked soon turned to a blistering fury. Her lovely features transformed her into a fuming siren. Without another word, she stamped off down the street, leaving Shad open mouthed. 'Where are you going?' he called after her.

'To have it out with that scheming rat,' she snapped back.

The last thing Shad needed was for this gutsy yet enthralling woman to challenge a ruthless bandit, who would not hesitate to chop her down to save his own skin, not to mention the payroll. He quickly caught up with her.

'Hold on there, Belle,' he said pulling her to a stop. She strove to free herself, but Shad was determined that she should not throw her life away unnecessarily. 'We need to think this through before rushing in without any plan. That critter is likely getting ready to quit the territory right now. You rushing in there like a rampant angel of vengeance is only gonna earn you a bullet. The scheming brigand might not have pulled the trigger, but as a member of the gang he sure is tarnished with all those killings. So he has nothing to lose in adding you to the list.'

The stark truth of Shad's observation finally paid off. Rationality overcame the stubborn inflexibility gripping her overwrought frame. 'Guess you're right,' she morosely admitted. 'I'm just so darned angry at that slimy toad making a fool of me like this. What are we going to do about it?'

'*You* are gonna do *nothing*,' Shad insisted firmly. 'This critter is dangerous, more so now that his whole plan is falling apart.' He held up a hand when she tried to object. 'Best thing you can do is just show me where he's stashed the wagon, then go back and book a room at The National Hotel. Wait for me there until I can join you.' With some reluctance she agreed to his proposal. 'We need to be careful if'n this business is gonna be solved without any more blood being spilled,' Shad emphasized, holding her with an intense gaze. 'So where is the show wagon being stored?'

'All I know is that he's taken it to a livery stable at the north end of town – a neighbourhood that respectable folks tend to avoid,' she declared. The girl could still barely credit why the showman had become involved with a gang of ruthless killers. 'I never figured he would stoop to this level. He always seemed so easygoing.'

'It only needs a guy like Rankin to come along and offer easy pickings for a gullible fool like him to have his head turned,' Shad sneered. 'Soon as I laid eyes on the locust, I knew he couldn't be trusted. Can you lead me down there?'

'We called here last year, so I should be able to find it,' Belle muttered thoughtfully, wrapping the shawl around her shoulders. Underneath she was still clad in the skimpy costume.

Shad checked his gun was fully loaded as they set off on what proved to be a tortuous search. Blackfoot was quite a large town, so it took some time of backtracking and searching before they eventually chanced upon the stable – proprietor: Malachi Dobbs. It was set back among a huddle of squalid shacks adjacent to a tannery on one side and a candlemaker on the other. The smell of the tannery alone was enough to keep people away.

'This must be it,' Belle excitedly declared. 'I recall the name Dobbs coming up in our conversations once.'

She was about to walk in through the open door when Shad pulled her back. 'Remember what I said. You keep out of this. Jumping in two-footed will alert him to our presence,' he warned keeping his voice low. 'Now you head off.'

She clung on to his arm, shooting a concerned look at his craggy face. 'Promise me you won't put your life in danger.' Her heart-felt plea brought a lump to Shad's throat. 'I didn't nurse you back to health for that critter to ruin all my good work.' They were standing close together. He could smell her musky womanhood – the earthy mix of sweat and perfume was heady, making him feel giddy, exhilarated. 'Promise me,' she repeated.

He didn't reply. Instead, taking her in his arms, he kissed her ardently on the lips. Her body yielded to his touch. For that brief moment nothing else mattered. But the reality of their situation soon intruded in the form of movement inside the stable. They grudgingly broke apart. 'Go now,' Shad whispered, pushing her away. 'And don't look back. The last thing I want now is any harm coming to you.'

# TWELVE

# BAD MEDICINE...

After making sure Belle did not change her mind, Shad carefully circled round the stable, looking for a safe entry point. A door on the far side opened at his touch. He slipped inside, pausing to listen for any suspicious sounds. The need for caution was challenged by a pungent stench of horse dung impossible to ignore. But movement in the front section of the stable indicated the distinct probability that Lavelle was getting ready to scarper.

He could see that the large double doors at the front were open, though he had no chance of reaching them due to a sturdy partition. The only access to that part of the stable was by a ladder into the hay loft. A horse whinnied as it was led out. This was followed by the slap of reins as the animal and its rider galloped off. Was this Lavelle disappearing with the loot?

There was only one way to find out. He quickly climbed the ladder, scuttling across the bales of hay. And there below was the medicine wagon, seemingly abandoned, with no horses in the traces. Nobody else was in the vicinity. To make certain this was indeed the case, he climbed down the far side and carefully circled around the gaudy contraption. A quick peak inside confirmed that it was empty. And to prove that his supposition had been correct, there was the heavy payroll box, the lid open and the contents removed.

Shad issued a lurid curse under his breath. By chance he was facing a window, and that was when he spotted movement behind him reflected in the glass. Somebody was sneaking up on him, obviously with the intention of doing him harm. Any normal person would have called out, demanding to know his business. Was it Lavelle? The other rider could have been an innocent customer.

Whoever it was needed stopping, and quickly if he was to continue breathing in this rancid air. He spun round, ready to confront the sly operator. And just in the nick of time, as a small jigger bearing a close resemblance to a starved rat lunged at him with a two-pronged pitchfork. Shad only had time to side-step, but was still pinioned by one of the prongs, which pierced his vest to the wagon. A sharp pain in his side indicated the lethal prong had drawn blood – another couple of inches and he would have been done for.

The attacker growled out a wild curse at having his ambush thwarted as he strove to drag the fork free, Shad's yelp of pain spurring him on to finish the job. Shad hung on to the shaft with one hand, wondering how to curb the maniac's aggression. Who could he be? The only answer that came to mind was the stable owner – Malachi Dobbs. He must have been paid a cut of the proceeds for his involvement in hiding the wagon. Lavelle and this jumpy varmint had to be old buddies for him to react in such a violent manner in neutralizing anybody sniffing around the wagon.

No words had been exchanged during the brief attempt to kill him, only a series of garbled grunts from the hostile Dobbs. None were needed in response. Shad knew the score: Ratty's job was to kill any snoopers, thus preventing a pursuit. The guy abandoned his tussle with the wedged pitchfork, and instead grabbed a nearby bucket to use as a bludgeon.

Only one response was possible under these circumstances. Shad drew his gun as the heavy bucket was raised. No opportunity had been granted to reason with the guy, so he was forced against his will to pull the trigger. The gun blasted, stopping the potential killer in his tracks. Another bullet in the guts ensured that Dobbs would not see the light of day again.

The noise in the confined space rattled Shad's eardrums. He sucked in a few gasps of the heavy air to settle his beating ticker. Having recovered his composure, he instantly regretted having to kill the skunk.

The terminal reaction had been instinctive, a matter of survival. But now he was left in a quandary. Only Ratface would have any notion as to where Lavelle was heading.

So where did that leave Shadrak Pickett's quest for retribution?

Then it struck him. Only one other person would be privy to that piece of vital information. Belle Sunbeam! Before leaving the stable to join her at The National Hotel, Shad dragged the dead ostler into a vacant stall and covered the body with straw. He had no fear that the gun shots would draw unwelcome attention in this part of the town. But neither did he want other customers stumbling upon his handiwork.

On returning to the main street, Shad casually entered the hotel. An enquiry as to the room occupied by Miss Sunbeam was not needed. The desk clerk was fast asleep, his boots resting on the counter. A glance at the line of keys hanging behind revealed that only two were missing, those to rooms nos 2 and 6. The others were either unoccupied or the residents were out. He quickly and silently ascended the central staircase, pausing first outside room no. 2. He knocked, and affecting a suitably foppish voice, announced, 'Message for Miss Sunbeam'. There was no response so he knocked again. The reply when it came was an acidic growl: 'Clear off. You've gotten the wrong room.'

'Sorry, sir,' Shad rejoined, 'My mistake' and then moved down the corridor to no. 6. Nobody else was about, so his firm knock was answered with a cautious 'Who's there, please?'

'It's me, Shad Pickett.' The door opened and he scuttled inside. Belle was standing there clad in a decidedly revealing negligée. All notions of his quest paled into insignificance, and all he wanted to do was take this girl in his arms. Then the grim reminder of how he had arrived at this nadir in his life came tumbling back into his head. Any feelings he harboured for Belle Sunbeam, any future they might have together, all depended on his bringing the perpetrators of his downfall to justice.

Before the girl could ask how his search of the stable had transpired, Shad blurted out that Lavelle had scarpered with the dough. No mention was made of his lethal encounter with Malachi Dobbs. Her startled look of shock saw a hand raised to her mouth. Fearful eyes were staring, wide as saucers. He then came straight to the point: 'Did Lavelle ever mention to you any special place he called home? Somewhere he might head for when he had acquired a grubstake to set him up for life?'

Belle's sylphlike features creased up in thought. For a long minute she remained still, racking her brains for the clue requested. The sands of time were steadily running down, and Shad tried to conceal his impatience. Then a light shone, bright as a full moon. She snapped her fingers, the answer bursting forth.

'A couple of times he did mention a place he had bought over in Wyoming territory,' she excitedly announced. Shad's whole body stiffened in anticipation. This was what he wanted to hear. 'When he was feeling a bit down in the mouth, fed up with playing the cheery purveyor of quack cures, he sometimes expressed a wish to pack it all in and head for this bolt hole. At first he wouldn't say where. But I managed to worm it out of him...'

She paused, smiling at Shad's gaping stare. 'It's called West Thumb, near to Yellowstone Lake.' Her head shook in recollection of the reason this never happened, as she continued: 'But there was never enough dough to satisfy him. Emile was a mite too fond of chancing his arm at the poker tables. And believe me, he was not a good player.'

Following this welcome piece of news, Shad's thoughts focused on the journey he would need to undertake. Yellowstone was renowned for its hot springs, most famous of which was Old Faithful, said to erupt skywards every fifty minutes. A beautiful place to be sure, according to reports from army patrols sent out to tackle the Crow Indians living in that locality. Lieutenant Pickett, unfortunately, had never been so detailed. He had, however, seen pictures in magazines extolling its scenic splendour.

But more apt, as far as Lavelle was concerned, was its remote location. Encompassed by snow-capped peaks, waterfalls and dense pine forests, this was a place where a lowlife of his ilk would feel safe from the law. Parts of the Yellowstone area occupied by the hostile Crows were safe for whites, as they were shunned by the Indians, who believed them to be haunted by evil spirits. West Thumb must be one.

The rough journey to the north-east entailed traversing the Grand Teton range. Shad would need to leave immediately if he were to catch up with the varmint before he hit the mountains. Much as he would have preferred to continue where their last emotional tryst had ended outside the stable, Shad knew that with every minute that passed, the sole remaining gang member was making good his getaway.

A brief clasp of bodies, a heart-felt plea from Belle to take care, then he forced his tingling frame to depart, assuring her that he would return safely. Whether that would happen was now in the hand of God, with a liberal assistance from his guardian angel.

# THIRTEEN

# ...MEANS NO CURE

Back in the stable with no interference, Shad was able to select a fine Barbary mare. Tough and reliable, with a calm temperament and the intelligence to sense its rider's expectations, the Barbary was the ideal horse for his journey. He helped himself to supplies from the dead ostler's storeroom, then hit the trail. The setting sun gave him the general direction to take. He was now in the lap of providence.

If Belle had been right in her assumption, then sooner or later he would find clues to Lavelle's movements. The guy would need to stop at trading posts to rest up and tend to his mount. And a Frenchman would be remembered. Hopefully that would be how Shad could track him down. On the second day out, he came across a remote outpost in Swan Valley on the left bend of the Snake River. There seemed

144

little doubt that the proprietor would recall a nattily dressed Frenchman.

When asked whether his quarry had passed through in the last few days, the suspicious instincts of the owner's Indian wife were immediately raised. 'I go fetch my husband,' she stammered out in Shoshone parlance. 'He will know.' She went into the back room to fetch the owner. Five minutes passed, then a burly jasper clad in a grimy apron appeared.

'Leaf on the Breeze says you been asking about a Frenchman passing through here,' he snapped out in a belligerent manner. 'What's your interest in this man?'

Shad immediately knew why this guy was acting so contrary. The accent gave it away. He was also French himself. What kind of bad luck was that? Declaring the truth was not going to produce any co-operation from this cynical frog. So he merely said, 'I need to catch up with him for personal reasons.'

'That ain't no explanation,' the critter said stubbornly. 'All types call here, many of them guys on the run from the law. They know that Honest Pierre can be trusted not to reveal their whereabouts.' That was when Leaf joined the self-proclaimed Honest Pierre and handed him a news-sheet, pointing to a picture and its report.

Once he had perused the article, he slapped it down on the counter, jabbing the picture with a greasy finger. A twisted lip made the ugly countenance even more demonic. 'You're Shad Pickett, the

disgraced officer drummed out of the army for cowardice!' The vitriolic accusation struck the victim like
a slap in the face. So intent was he on catching up
with Lavelle he had clean forgotten that he was now
a universal pariah. The other patrons of the establishment had ceased their card game, and all eyes were
now focused on the defiled newcomer. Even here, in
this remote wilderness, Shad's besmeared reputation
had seen fit to haunt him. 'Think you can come in
here seeking to tarnish an innocent traveller? Get out
of here, Pickett! Your kind ain't welcome at Honest
Pierre's!'

Silence followed as half-a-dozen pairs of hostile
eyes drilled into the outcast's back as he made his way
out. He turned at the door. 'At least tell me if'n I'm
on the right trail for the Yellowstone,' he pleaded,
appealing to some smidgen of sympathy from these
hard-faced men.

One cowboy, younger than the others, piped up:
'Keep heading north of east for the Tetons, and you'll
make it in four or five days.'

Shad nodded his thanks to the speaker, who
received some less than cordial looks from his pals.
The kid ignored them. 'My brother suffered the same
fate for cowering in a foxhole during an attack by
the Sioux in Montana. He never recovered, and shot
himself six months later. He was only sixteen.' That
tough disclosure from the plucky cowpoke effectively
silenced the muttered griping. 'Don't let it happen to
you, mister.'

'Don't you be helping out a yeller skunk that ran out on his buddies, Little Mick,' a heavy-set bruiser snapped out. 'He don't deserve any help from us Box Elder boys.'

He may have been a pint-sized puncher, but Little Mick Garrity was no pushover. He threw a piercing look towards Nevada Jones, who was foreman of the spread. 'You can give orders out on the range, boss,' he replied in a level tone, 'but not here.'

'Much obliged for your understanding, fella,' Shad commended the youngster. 'It took guts for you to admit that. I'll make sure to take your advice.' A tip of his hat followed in acknowledgement of the support.

As he was leaving Mick turned his attention back to the victim of the animosity. 'You'll find a short cut over the Snake Gorge by a rope bridge. Look out for Elephant Butte when you've crossed the plains,' the helpful kid called after him. 'You can't miss it, high up on the rim. The bridge crosses a gorge on the far side.'

Like this kid, there were clearly folks out there who would not judge him badly. But the truth was that the Little Micks of this world were few and far between. The vast majority of encounters would be like those of Rockerbox Riley, Buck Anders and Honest Pierre. He sucked in a deep breath and wandered across to where his horse was patiently waiting.

The Barbary had been chewing on some hay left outside especially for customers stopping off at the trading post. So she was fully rejuvenated and raring

147

to go. Having been denied a stay for the night Shad wanted to put some distance behind him before bedding down in his bedroll. A hard night under the stars with beef jerky and sourdough biscuits was a poor second to hot food and a soft mattress. Was this going to be his lot wherever he chanced to stop? The thought spurred him on.

The horse appeared to sense her new rider's determination, and immediately picked up the pace. Ahead of him, the sharply honed peaks of the Tetons appeared dark and forbidding as the dark shadows of evening spread their tentacles across the bleak landscape. The stark landmark shaped like an elephant's head was a sure guide.

That night he camped out on the edge of a deep ravine beside a rope bridge spanning the mighty Snake River far below. High up in the foothills he spent a cold night huddled in his blanket. Sleep was long in coming as the thought of his quest and how it would conclude kept impinging on his mind. Eventually the dreamy recollection of Belle Sunbeam's glorious countenance lulled him into the arms of Orpheus.

He was up at the crack of dawn as a watery sun rose above the turrets of rock in the east. That was when the rickety nature of the bridge presented itself. Narrow with slatted crosspieces, it was supported by thick rope cables dipping across the ravine, anchored at each side by substantial beams. It had clearly not been built for the passage of four-legged transport.

The question Shad was asking himself was – if Lavelle was heading for Yellowstone country, had he come this way? A close examination of the immediate locality revealed no hoofprints, only the prints of moccasins worn by the Indian builders, probably Shoshone. So maybe Lavelle had taken a longer way round to find a better crossing point downstream. He had clearly not received the helpful directions from that young cowpoke at Honest Pierre's. Little Mick and his buddies must also have traversed this bridge at some point for him to have suggested it.

Girding himself up for the crossing, Shad gingerly led the Barbary on to the narrow bridge. It swayed and shook under the extra weight. He paused, drawing breath and hoping he had made the right decision, before commencing the risky traverse. Slowly but surely, step by step, man and beast made their cautious way over the deep gorge. Shad made a point of not looking down. Once the halfway point had been passed he began to breathe more easily.

When finally back on solid ground he sat down and gulped in a lungful of clear, relief-giving air. He had made it. Only then did he sidle to the edge and peer down into the huge gash carved out by the sinuous course of the aptly name Snake River, soon disappearing from view round the next bend. Far below, a thin white line indicated its passage northwards into the distance.

Shad mounted up and pointed the faithful Barbary away from the gorge towards the north-east. Two days later he was following the rim of a cliff face overlooking the Teton Valley when he spotted a lone rider far below. Could this be his quarry? He drew the horse to a halt and extracted his army spyglass from the saddle bag. Adjusting the focus he homed in on the rider. A sharp intake of breath made his heart race on recognizing the odious figure of Emile Lavelle. That tall blue hat was unmistakeable.

The route by way of Elephant Butte had got him ahead of the rat. He patted the horse's neck. 'This is all down to you and Little Mick,' he remarked with a smile angling the horse down a narrow trail through the dense flank of ponderosa pine cloaking the valley sides. 'Now all we have to do is catch the critter.'

As the duo descended the mountain side, gaps in the tree cover revealed that they were slowly closing the distance separating them from the fleeing brigand. The steeply winding trail necessitated extreme care to avoid a tumble. That was when the Barbary came into her own. Shad allowed the fine horse to pick her own path, safe in the knowledge that she would not unseat him.

A half hour later and they had reached valley level. Shad was confident that he had come out ahead of the sticky-fingered showman. Now all he needed was to find the perfect spot to prescribe his own dose of medicine. He found it within minutes: a cluster of trees through which the valley trail ran. Tying off the Barbary out of sight, he waited until the approaching rider was spotted a mile distant before shimmying up

a tree. Then he edged along a solid branch overhang-
ing the line the rider would take.

And there he crouched. Hidden by the leafy
boughs awaiting his destiny. Seconds, minutes, hours
seemed to pass before the steady thud of hoof beats
broke the stillness. The moment was at hand. The
avenger gritted his teeth, preparing himself to drop
down on to the passing rider. He prayed that fortune
was on his side. The guy needed to pass immediately
below where he was concealed.

Louder and louder grew the approaching thrum of
hooves, sounding like a runaway locomotive career-
ing down a grade. And then he saw him, riding at the
trot but slightly askew. Shad edged across to the limit
of the branch hoping it would not shake and alert his
quarry. The man's face was hidden by the silly hat. No
doubt he was musing on how he was going to spend
all his ill-gotten gains.

Then he was passing beneath the tree. Shad judged
that he would make his drop just before the guy
reached him. He landed on the back of the horse,
much to the rider's total confusion. 'Aaaaaagh!
Sacré bleu!!' The French epithet burst forth as the
assailant dragged him backwards off the horse. Both
men hit the ground hard. The top hat rolled away
in the dust. But it was the attacker who recovered
first. Jumping to his feet he slammed a bunched fist
into the Frenchman's jutting chin. Lavelle staggered
back against the tree trunk. Blood dribbled from a
cut lip.

But he was not finished yet. There was too much at stake, twenty thousand in greenbacks to be precise. He growled out another incoherent bout of foreign curses while scrambling behind the tree leaving Shad exposed, out in the open. 'You again,' he snarled on recognizing his pursuer. He had no idea how the unwelcome passenger had managed to track him down. Nor was he bothered. All Lavelle cared about was saving his own skin and snuffing out this interfering locust.

He reached into his pocket and withdrew the small pocket pistol. 'You should not have stuck your nose where it is not wanted. Now you pay the price.' The gun spat flame and hot lead twice. The first shot missed its target. But the second creased Shad's arm. Luckily it was his left. He backed off, scrabbling behind a tree on the opposite side of the trail. Another two bullets whined off the trunk.

Shad's hat had remained glued to his head. He now removed it and gingerly held it out. A frosty smile revealed gleaming teeth as two more bullets were aimed at the hat. 'Aaaaargh!' cried the 'victim' as the hat fell to the ground. The oldest trick in the book and it had worked. Six bullets and six empty cartridges equals an empty pistol. A shout of triumph rang out from behind the other tree as Lavelle jumped out from cover, convinced he had killed his antagonist.

Witnessing Shad casually emerging from his own cover saw the greenhorn gunslinger raising his pistol to finish the job. Acute shock was exhibited on the smarmy countenance. Cocking and firing on empty chambers merely produced inert clicks. Only then did he know he had been duped. The gun was thrown at Shad's head but he easily avoided it. 'You should have stuck with the medicine show, Napoleon,' the advancing avenger scoffed. 'Money, as they say, is the root of all evil. And your greedy ambitions are gonna see you breaking rocks on a chain gang.'

Lavelle was not about to surrender, having come this far. Only then did the Frenchman reveal his *pièce de résistance*, a small gun hidden up his sleeve. It must have been on a spring mechanism designed for just such an emergency as this. Clearly the ruse had not been employed for some time, as Lavelle fumbled with the single-shot Remington. That gave Shad the chance to draw his own revolver, throwing himself to one side as both weapons barked together.

The .30 calibre bullet from the Remington buzzed Shad's ear, clipping the skin. His own shot was more accurate, striking the greenhorn in the throat. The brief contest was over, blood spurting from a ruptured artery as Lavelle's glazed eyes rolled up into his head. The winner stood there, alone on that trail, his gun resting against his leg. Smoke twined from the barrel as his gaze fastened on to the dead form.

Shock paralysed his system, just like it always did following a brutal conflict. In the heat of battle, the innate sense of survival keeps a man going. Only

153

later, when it's all over, does the grim truth of taking life hit home. Though in this case only momentarily. Emile Lavelle, if not a killer himself, was responsible by association for many deaths. His avaricious inclination had led to a sudden and brutal demise for which Shad Pickett felt no guilt.

He looked across at the man's horse standing idly chewing on a clump of gramma grass some fifty yards up the trail. It was the saddle bags that were of most interest. He hurried across and quickly ascertained that the stolen payroll was indeed crammed inside the twin leather carriers. His fingers riffled through the tightly packed bundles of notes. A huge sense of relief flooded through his wiry frame.

But it was not over yet. There was still the tricky matter of securing Jake Rankin's release from the Blackfoot jail. How would a tough lawman like Grit Angstrum react to Shad's request for the killer's transfer back to Fort Wisdom?

# FOURTEEN

# INNOCENT AND GUILTY

Moments after the corpse of the medicine man had been hoisted back on to his horse and tied down, the first droplets of rain bounced off Shad's hat. In all the confusion occasioned by Lavelle's confrontation, he had failed to notice the gathering clouds tumbling down from the north. Within minutes the heavens opened. Shad managed to don his slicker before the full force of the storm made its presence felt. The Barbary remained impervious to the withering onslaught. Only a twitch of the ears displayed any hint of it bothering her.

Flashes of lighting forking down were quickly followed by ear-wrenching crashes of thunder. Yet still the horse remained steady as a rock, allowing her new master to mount up. Shad pulled his hat down,

turning round to head back the way he had come.
He couldn't help pondering on whether this was
an omen of the trouble he might encounter from
the Blackfoot lawman. But for now all his concen-
tration had to be on navigating a course back to the
town. The cloud base had dropped significantly, the
wall of rain blotting out the surrounding terrain.
The army compass offered a vital advantage in this
respect, enabling him to steer the Barbary in the
right direction.

The closer he drew to his destination, the more
anxious he became about the reception when he
arrived. Even though the storm had passed over,
problems still loomed large in his mind. Honest
Pierre's place was bypassed. All he had to look forward to was seeing Belle Sunbeam's smiling face.
Then he remembered the written confession dictated to Pastor Amory. He drew the Barbary to a halt
and took it out of his pocket, once again perusing
the cogent message.

Surely the stark fact that Jake Rankin could not
have ridden from Arco Butte to the settler's home
in one day would sway his decision. It was a journey that would take a fast rider at least three days.
Any reasonable person would have to accept this
confession as proof that he was innocent of Lucy
Karlsson's murder. He could only hope that Grit
Angstrum was such a guy. The notion spurred
him on.

156

Three days later he was riding down the main street of Blackfoot. His destination was the sheriff's office. Even though he wanted to see Belle, Shad was anxious to present his theory to the lawman and secure Jake Rankin's release into his custody. His arrival with the medicine man strapped over his saddle caused a distinct stir. A crowd gathered round the newcomer eager to hear what had happened.

In the heat of the moment Shad had completely forgotten his own ignominy in the eyes of the populace. It came as a surprise, therefore, when some avid newsreader called out: 'That's the guy who was cashiered from the army for cowardice!' All eyes turned towards the rider dismounting in front of the law office. 'Yeh, I read about that in the *Idaho Journal*,' another reader declared. 'He ran away and let some thieving gang kill the troopers under his command, the yellow rat!'

Within minutes, Shad was being roughly jostled by the crowd. 'He deserves to get his neck stretched along with that other killer in the jail.' That suggestion elicited a howl of agreement. Once again, the ugly mood of vigilante law was threatening to blow up in Blackfoot. It was fortunate for the object of their anger that he was close to the jail.

The noise soon brought Grit Angstrum hurrying out of the door. 'What in thunderation is going on out here?' he demanded, toting the shotgun. The previous incursion was clearly still very much on his mind.

'We've caught that yellow belly in the paper who dished his buddies,' was the reply from one of the more vociferous participants.

'And he's brought in that showman, dead as a doornail,' another spat out.

The sheriff's eyes twitched. But he was not about to have another riot on his hands. 'I'll take care of this,' he snapped, fixing a menacing eye on the ringleaders. 'There'll be no repetition of what happened before.' Deputy Flick Gallatin had now joined him. Together they presented a steadfast front of determination. He signalled for Shad to get inside the jail. He needed no second bidding. 'Now get about your business while I find out what's happened.' And with that he backed off inside the jail.

Shad wasted no time in succinctly but accurately relaying all the main facts, boldly emphasizing his own innocence of the accusation brought against him. 'It was that skunk languishing in your jail who is the cause of all my troubles,' he stressed. 'But he isn't the one who killed Lucy Karlsson. That critter is an outlaw called Bucktooth Axell. Foo Chang at the Wayfarer is holding him for you to arrest.'

The sheriff had listened intently to the disclosure. It sure was a mighty strange tale. Scepticism as to its validity was evident on his warped features. 'I can prove that Rankin is innocent,' Shad avidly assured the lawman, hooking out the confession, which he handed over. 'No way could the critter have killed Karlsson when he was already at Arco Butte with me. He caught me flat-footed there. But I need him alive to take back to Fort Wisdom.'

He waited anxiously for the doughty sheriff to make his decision. 'I ain't doubting your story about this rat tricking you so as to throw the blame for that robbery elsewhere. But how do I know this confession wasn't written by you?'

It was Flick Gallatin who offered an answer. 'Let me see that, Sheriff,' he said stepping forwards. 'My pa supplies Kloot Amory with the liquor for his saloon. I'd know his writing anywhere from the order form he sends.' The deputy then carefully studied the confession. Shad was on tenterhooks as he read it through. 'It's his writing sure enough. No mistake. This confession is genuine.'

Shad visibly relaxed. Now it was all up to the sheriff. 'Reckon we appear to have the wrong man in there. So there ain't no reason to hold him. He's all your'n, mister. And I wish you luck in securing an exoneration. No man wants to be labelled a coward.' He then ordered his deputy to go arrest the real killer being held at The Wayfarer saloon under the watchful eye of Foo Chang.

In something of a daze, Shad left the jail and headed over to The National Hotel and that much anticipated liaison with Belle. For the first time in too long his step was light, his mood buoyant. What the future might hold he had no idea. But with Belle by his side life could surely only be on the way up. And to give added credence to this most fervent wish, there she was on the steps outside the hotel waving to him, a glorious smile matching the brilliance of the noonday sun.